Rough & Rugged Lily

Other Books Available

The Lily Series

Here's Lily!

Lily Robbins, M.D. (Medical Dabbler)

Lily and the Creep

Lily's Ultimate Party

Ask Lily

Lily the Rebel

Lights, Action, Lily!

Lily Rules!

Rough & Rugged Lily

Lily Speaks!

Horse Crazy Lily

Lily's Church Camp Adventure

Lily's Passport to Paris

Lily's in London?!

Nonfiction

The Beauty Book

The Body Book

The Buddy Book

The Best Bash Book

The Blurry Rules Book

The It's MY Life Book

The Creativity Book

The Uniquely Me Book

The Year 'Round Holiday Book

The Values & Virtues Book

The Fun-Finder Book

The Walk-the-Walk Book

Dear Diary

Girlz Want to Know

NIV Young Women of Faith Bible

YWOF Journal: Hey! This Is Me

Take It from Me

Rough & Rugged Lily

Nancy Rue

Zonderkidz

Zonder**kidz**®

The children's group of Zondervan

www.zonderkidz.com

Rough & Rugged Lily
Copyright © 2002 by Women of Faith

Requests for information should be addressed to:
Zonderkidz, *Grand Rapids, Michigan 49530*

ISBN: 0-310-70260-7

Published in association with the literary agency of Alive Communications, Inc., 7680 Goddard Street, Suite 200, Colorado Springs, CO 80920.

Editor: Barbara Scott
Interior design: Amy Langeler
Art direction: Michelle Lenger
Printed in the United States of America

04 05 06 /❖ DC/ 11 10 9 8 7 6

Chapter 1

This is gonna be way cool," Lily said.

She squirmed around under her seatbelt so she could see Suzy and Reni in the backseat. They were both nodding, and even in the darkness of the van, she could tell both pairs of dark eyes were shining with that kind of delight that appears only when something really neat is about to happen.

"I didn't think we'd get to do anything this big in *Junior* Youth Group," Reni said, the beads on her numerous braids clacking together as she shook her head. "I thought they only did stuff like camp-outs in the *Senior* group."

"Is it gonna be that big, I mean, really?" Suzy said.

Lily didn't have to be able to see her to know her eyebrows were coming together in a worry knot. She'd wondered how long it would take nervous little Suzy to start stressing about this—but Lily was ready for her.

"It's gonna be major big," Lily said. She loosened her seatbelt a little so she could get up on her knees and peer at her two friends over the seat.

"You heard them say this is gonna be total 'survival in the wild,'" Reni put in.

"But there's nothing to worry about. You saw those people who are gonna head it up—they're professionals. And besides, they're gonna be training us from now 'til March, which is—"

"Three months," Reni said.

"So it's gonna be fine." Lily gave her head of curly red hair a final nod. She could see Suzy nodding, too, though with less enthusiasm. Suzy wasn't a go-at-everything-full-blast person. Lily was already envisioning herself pitching a tent up in the Poconos, fully prepared to ward off an entire family of bears.

"I'm glad we've got three months to get ready," Reni said. "I'm gonna have to do some *major* talking to get my dad to fork over for all that camping equipment. Did you see all that stuff they had up there on the stage?"

"But they said we didn't have to buy all that," Suzy said. "They said we should just be looking in our garages and attics for stuff."

"My parents don't *have* stuff," Reni said. "They've never been camping in their lives!"

For the first time since they'd left the church parking lot, Lily turned to look at her father, who was driving the van—and probably writing his next lecture on C. S. Lewis in his head. As she looked at his slender, freckled hands on the steering wheel and his I'm-dreaming-of-*The-Chronicles-of-Narnia* eyes peering through the icy windshield, it occurred to Lily that she might have the same problem.

"Do *we* have any camping equipment around the house, Dad?" she said.

Dad pulled the van to a stop at a red light and looked at her as if he'd just realized she was in the car with him. "Do we have *what*, Lilliputian?" he said. The heater wasn't working too well in the van, and the "what" came out with a puff of frosty breath.

"Camping equipment," Lily said.

"Why?" Dad said. "Are you planning to run away from home?"

Lily rolled her eyes at Suzy and Reni, who giggled into their mittened hands. Dad had *so* not heard a word they'd been saying—and it didn't take a nuclear physicist to figure out that there wasn't so much as a tent stake anywhere *near* the Robbins' house.

"I'll ask Mom," she said. "I bet she camped before you guys got married."

Dad chuckled. "She tried to drag me out into the wild once, but I managed to escape."

That was good for more eye rolling.

"Ooh—look at *those* lights!" Reni said.

Reni was clearing a circle in the fog on the side window. Lily craned her neck to see what she was pointing at. It was pretty hard to miss. Somebody's yard was so lit up that it looked as if the sky had snowed twinkle lights.

"We saw that the other night," Suzy said. "My dad said he'd hate to see their electric bill."

"Yeah," Reni said. "My dad lets my mom hang a wreath on the door and that's it for outside decorations. He's always whining about money."

"Wow," was all Lily said. When it came to Christmas, *her* parents never mentioned how much it was costing. Christmas at the Robbins' house was a huge deal. They didn't go as all-out with the lights as some people did, but there was usually the manger scene on the lawn and the candles in every window—not to mention the platter after platter of cookies that came out of the kitchen, and the ten-foot tree they always put up, and the pile of presents that magically appeared under it on Christmas Eve.

But then another thought occurred to her. It was only six days 'til Christmas—school was already out for vacation—and *nothing* had magically appeared at their house.

Yikes, Lily thought, *I haven't even made my wish list yet!*

That part wasn't surprising. Until Friday—and this was only Sunday—she'd been wrapped up in the business of being seventh-grade class president, and talk about a big deal. She and the other officers had thrown the party to end all parties for their class the last day before the holidays. No wonder she hadn't noticed that nary a cookie had yet made its way out of the oven.

Besides all that, Mom and Dad were trying to adopt another kid, which meant filling out forms and going to meetings, and the house was overrun with construction workers, who were adding on a new room to the place. Nobody had had time to squeeze in Christmas preparations.

But Lily smiled to herself as she watched the front-yard displays of lights flicker by. This was perfect timing. She would make her wish list right away and fill it with all that neat stuff the survival camp people had shown them.

It's a good thing I hadn't already written it, she thought, *because I would have loaded it up with outfits to wear to conduct class meetings. I've got stuff I can use for that—but I do* not *have a sleeping bag, a tent, a canteen, decent hiking boots, and—*

"Is this your street, Suzy-Q?" Dad said.

Lily shook herself out of her camping dreams as Dad rounded the corner by Suzy's house. "Hey, you guys," she said, swiveling around once more to face Suzy and Reni. "I'm gonna ask for camping equipment for Christmas. Have you already given your parents your wish lists?"

"My what?" Suzy said.

"Your list of what you want for Christmas."

"Oh." Suzy gave a nervous giggle. "We don't do that. We just circle all the stuff we want in the catalogs. All that has to be ordered. So I did it at Thanksgiving."

"I already did mine, and there's stuff under the tree already," Reni said. She shrugged. "But I can always ask for more stuff. That's the best thing about being an only child."

Lily thought about her two brothers and shook her head. "Trust me, that's not the *best* thing," she said.

The van stopped in Suzy's driveway, and as she slid the door open, the light came on—revealing not only Suzy and Reni but also the van's usual tangle of junk mail, left-behind gloves, and McDonald's bags. Even though Suzy had to shake a dried-up French fry off of her knitted cap before she pulled it onto her head, she was smiling. "That's still a good idea, though, Lily," she said. "My birthday's in January."

"Get you an L. L. Bean catalog, girl!" Reni said.

"Merry Christmas, everybody, in case I don't see you," Suzy said.

Reni and Lily said "Merry Christmas" back. Dad, Lily noticed, was unusually quiet. As he backed out of the driveway, she saw that his eyes were bright and focused, and Lily searched the last few minutes to make sure she hadn't said anything dumb. Dad concentrating on the present moment was usually a sure sign that she had.

Reni didn't seem to notice. "You know what would be cool?" she said to Lily. "If we could get matching sleeping bags and backpacks."

"All the Girlz!" Lily said. "'Cause we're gonna bring Kresha and Zooey as guests, right?"

"Ye-ah," Reni said, as if Lily had just asked her if the sun would be coming up tomorrow. "I think I'll ask for a six-person tent so there'll be room enough for all of us *and* all our junk."

"So that means I don't have to put a tent on my list. I'll ask for one of those rain ponchos instead."

"Definitely. Oh—this is my street, Dr. Robbins," Reni said.

Dad just kind of grunted. The fact that he didn't call her Renoir or Reindeer or one of his other pet names for Reni made Lily a little uneasy. Something was definitely up.

"Call me tomorrow and read me your list," Reni was saying as she plowed through the assorted junk and climbed out of the backseat. "We have to get coordinated."

Lily held up a knit-clad thumb.

"Merry Christmas, Dr. Robbins," Reni said.

"Same to you, Reni," Dad said. And that was all.

In fact, that was all the entire way home, and that *never* happened. Lily and her dad could always find something to chatter back and forth about. They were alike that way, which made sense to Lily since they also looked alike. Lily and her older brother Art had both gotten Dad's curly hair and pale skin and eyes that could look right into people, or so their younger brother Joe often pointed out. "It creeps me out when she looks at me like that," he would say.

Right now, Lily could see what he meant. Although Dad didn't say a word as they drove home, he gave Lily a few looks that made her want to shout, "*What?* What did I do?"

But even though she racked her brain the rest of the way and continued to when she was propped up in bed with her prayer journal and Otto, her little dog, and didn't stop after the light was out and she was curled up with Otto behind her knees, she couldn't figure out what it was that had plunged Dad into silence. It was like waiting for that last drop of ketchup to come out of the bottle.

It finally came to her the next morning as she started compiling her Christmas wish list before the sleep was even out of her eyes.

It was all that talk about Christmas in the car, she thought as she chose just the right gel pen for the job. *It made Dad feel bad because he and Mom haven't done anything about it yet.*

He wouldn't feel bad for long, she was sure, once she gave him *and* Mom the nudge. She got busy without even putting on slippers or going down to raid the refrigerator, and she was about halfway through with the list when she heard Art's music go on above her in his attic room. Art was a major musician in high school, and he always hit the play button on his CD player before he even opened his eyes.

"He better open 'em quick," Lily said to Otto, who was yawning and beginning to move from his place at the end of Lily's bed. "All *three* of us have got to give Mom and Dad the nudge."

Lily hurried out into the hall. Joe was just coming out of the bathroom, clad in a Philadelphia Eagles jersey that was six times too big for his scrawny ten-year-old body. He saw Lily and clapped his hands to the side of his face.

"Yikes! What is it?" he said.

"Oh, and you're a vision in the morning yourself," Lily said dryly. "Did you make your wish list yet?"

"I wish you'd get a face transplant."

"No—moron—your Christmas wish list."

Joe put his hand on Lily's arm, sadly shaking his head. Lily could feel her eyes narrowing in suspicion.

"I gotta tell ya somethin', Lil," he said.

"What?"

"There's no such thing as Santa Claus."

Lily jerked her arm away and proceeded toward the steps that led to the attic. "Fine," she said. "Go without presents this year. I'm making my list, though, because in case you haven't picked up on it, nobody seems to be doing anything about Christmas around here."

"Oh," Joe said.

He did look a little baffled, and as Lily started up the steps, he called after her, "You got any paper I could use?"

Art was already on the phone when Lily knocked on his door and let herself in. He'd probably slept with it, and he was more than likely talking to Marsha, his girlfriend of the week. Lily made a throat-slitting motion with her finger.

"What?" Art mouthed. He was still too sleepy to act annoyed.

"We have to talk about Christmas," she whispered.

He pantomimed writing as he continued to murmur into the phone. Lily snatched up his school binder from the floor, ripped out a piece of paper, and wrote in big letters with a stub of a pencil, *Have you made your Christmas gift list for Mom and Dad?*

Art's eyes widened as he looked at it, and he nodded, although it was hard to tell whether he was nodding for Marsha or her. It became clear when he grabbed the pencil stub from Lily and wrote: *Speakers for my car; gift certificate for Tower Records* as he kept muttering "Uh-huh, uh-huh" into the receiver. Lily smiled and left.

Lily finished her list a few minutes later and decorated its envelope with a glitter pen.

It's a little longer than last year's, she thought as she took it downstairs to put it on Dad's desk. *But I did say on there that they could just give me a gift certificate to Camping World. They don't have to go out and do a bunch of shopping—I'm old enough not to expect a pile of wrapped presents under the tree.*

Dad wasn't in his study yet, so Lily left the envelope on his desk and was headed for the kitchen to see if Joe had eaten the last of the Fruity Pebbles when the doorbell rang. Lily looked ruefully down at her pjs and bare feet, but a peek out the window made it okay. It was Kresha and Zooey.

"What are you guys doing out so early?" Lily said as she opened the front door to a blast of freezing air and two red-cheeked faces.

"Presents!" Kresha said.

She pulled a lopsided package from behind her back and held it out, grinning. There was a hole in the end of each index finger of her gloves, so that two raw-looking fingers poked out. The fact that the gloves were two different colors didn't surprise Lily. Kresha wasn't known for her fashion sense.

Zooey was color-coordinated from head to toe in bright red and forest green—except for her lips, which were a pale shade of blue.

"You gotta be freezing," Lily said. "Come in!"

Zooey only barely got inside the door when she too pulled out a present.

"For me?" Lily said.

"No," Kresha said. "For the dog." Then she grinned her mischievous grin and threw both arms around Lily's neck. Since Kresha was still learning English—she was Croatian—she got a big kick out of herself when she made a joke in it.

"I haven't gotten you guys anything yet," Lily said as they trailed her into the living room. "I haven't had a chance to even go shopping."

"We didn't shop either," Zooey said. "We made these."

By the time they sat down on the couch, Kresha was so excited she practically had her gift for Lily unwrapped already, so it didn't take much to get it open the rest of the way. What was hard was figuring out just what it was.

Lily held up the ball of fabric tied with a ribbon at the top like a small sack and gazed at it.

"Smell it," Zooey whispered to her.

"Oh," Lily said, and took a big whiff.

It smelled like the mothballs her grandmother used in her coat closet, but Lily resisted the urge to cough and instead hugged Kresha's neck.

"Thanks, Kresh," she said. "I'll really get a lot of use out of this."

"Open mine," Zooey said.

Lily popped the tape on the tiny box Zooey handed her and lifted the lid. Two blue buttons stared up at her. Lily felt herself blinking.

"Put on, Lily!" Kresha shrieked, and snatched the buttons out of the box.

Only when she poked them at Lily's earlobes did Lily realize they were earrings.

"I got the idea out of a magazine," Zooey said. "And you always look good in blue."

"These are great," Lily said. She put her fingers up to feel them, and the button on the left dropped into her lap.

"It came unglued!" Zooey said. "And I even used Superglue!"

"I can fix it," Lily said. "Don't worry about it."

Zooey looked so distraught, Lily groped for a change of subject.

"So—what do you guys want for Christmas—I mean, from your parents?" she said.

"Candy!" Kresha said.

"That's it?" Lily said.

Zooey nudged her. "They do things different in Croatia," she whispered—as if Kresha couldn't hear her.

"In America we ask for presents—you know, like, *things*," Lily said to Kresha. "And I think you guys should both ask for camping equipment."

Before the questions could start, Lily launched into a description of the Junior Youth Group Survival Camp-Out. She couldn't help casting herself in the role of Outdoor Woman, because she'd thought of almost nothing else since last night. Even as she talked, she thought of a few more things she could have put on her list. Too bad her birthday was in May—

"Will you really get all that stuff?" Zooey said when Lily was finished.

"Well, yeah," Lily said. "It's Christmas. Don't you get what you put on your list?"

Zooey's big gray eyes looked blank. "What list?" she said.

"Tent costs much money?" Kresha said.

"It depends on what you get," Lily said—with authority. "The guy said you can get them as cheap as fifty dollars."

Kresha and Zooey gasped.

"I don't think I can go on this camping thing," Zooey said. "That's *way* too much money for my parents. I don't think all my presents together cost fifty dollars!"

"Oh," Lily said.

A stiff kind of silence fell around the couch. Lily was glad when Dad stuck his head in the door from the dining room and said, "Lily— when you get free, we need to have a little family meeting."

Zooey shot up from the couch as if she'd been bitten in the behind.

"We'll go," she whispered, as Dad disappeared from the doorway. "He looked kinda mad."

Yeah, Lily thought after Zooey and Kresha had hurried out the front door. *He kinda did.*

Chapter 2

Mom and Joe were already in the family room when Lily followed her dad in there. Joe was looking longingly at the remote control, but he wasn't lunging for it, which meant Mom had already decreed there would be no TV during the meeting. When Art trailed in carrying the portable phone, Mom and Dad gave him such pointed looks that he put it on the table next to the remote with no argument. Yeah, the air was definitely tense.

"Whatever it is," Joe said, tucking his long legs up under the Eagles jersey, "I didn't do it."

"You *all* did it," Mom said. She held up two folded pieces of paper and an envelope, which Lily recognized as her Christmas list.

"I'm sorry they're late," Lily said. "I know it doesn't give you guys much time to shop, but like it says on mine, you can just give me a gift certificate."

"Same here," Art said.

"Cool," Joe said. "That leaves you plenty of time to shop for *my* stuff." He smiled the twitchy smile he inherited from his mom. "I'll even go with you if you want."

"There's barely enough time between now and *next* Christmas to buy all this," Mom said. She shook out one of the pieces of paper, which was crammed on both sides with Joe's early cursive.

"Jo-oe!" Lily said. "Talk about greedy."

"You had just as much on yours, Lil," Mom said. "You just write smaller."

Art snapped his fingers. "Man—I knew I shoulda typed mine."

"Are you three listening to yourselves?" Dad said.

It wasn't really the kind of question you answered. It was the kind of question that made you wish it had never been asked, especially coming from a usually forgetful, mild-mannered father. Lily chewed on her lower lip.

"We do kinda sound like a bunch of greedy little monsters," Art said.

"Speak for yourself!" Joe said.

"He's speaking for all of you." Dad shifted his blue eyes from Joe to Art to Lily and then, surprisingly, down to his hands, which were folded between his spread-apart knees as he leaned forward, arms on his thighs. He didn't look mad anymore. He looked—embarrassed.

"I don't know what we expected, though," he went on. "We've been filling your Christmas orders like we're Sears catalog ever since you were little. We've gone into debt every December to give you everything you've wanted—because you're such good kids—and every year the orders have been getting bigger and bigger. And we've allowed it."

"Now that we're no longer doing the credit card thing," Mom said, "we've suddenly realized that it's gotten out of control."

"No problem," Art said. He held out his hand to Mom. "Just give us back our lists, and we'll cut them in half."

"In half?" Joe said. Art shot him a look, and Joe immediately nodded. "At least in half," he said.

But Mom didn't hand over the lists. She exchanged glances with Dad—a sure sign that there was more to come.

"It isn't just the gifts—it's an entire attitude that we're not happy with," Dad said.

"What attitude?" Art said. "I haven't pulled a 'tude in a long time. I'm so over that stage."

"I'm not talking about a general 'tude," Dad said. And then, to Lily's horror, he looked right at her. "I'm talking about the kind of thing I heard in the van last night."

"I shoulda known it was you, Lily," Joe said.

"What the Sam Hill did you say?" Art said.

Lily looked helplessly at Dad. He shook his head. "It wasn't just Lily. It was Reni and Suzy—and you two characters—"

"We weren't even there!" Joe wailed.

"It's pervasive in your generation."

"I can't be 'pervasive'!" Joe said. "I don't even know what it is!"

"It means in today's society there's a lot of selfishness going on," Mom said. "And a lot of materialism. You know that one, Joe?"

"Yeah," Joe said. He scowled.

"Okay—so how do we make up for it?" Art said. "What's our punishment?"

Mom and Dad looked at each other again. Lily closed her eyes and saw not only all her camping equipment disappearing but also her entire Christmas vacation happening in the confines of her room.

"It's not the kind of thing you punish," Dad said. "It's the kind of thing you change. Your mother and I have decided that we are going

19

to have a different kind of Christmas this year—one that will teach us *all* something about ourselves."

Joe's big brown doe eyes narrowed so that he looked less like his usual Bambi and more like the evil hunter. Art, too, was looking suspicious. Lily felt her heart sinking.

I don't want different! she wanted to holler. *I like Christmas just the way it's always been!*

"Here's the plan," Dad said, and then he nodded at Mom.

"Bright and early tomorrow morning," Mom said, "we're leaving for North Carolina."

"How long are we gonna be gone?" Art said, nervously eyeing the phone.

"Your father has a professor friend who owns a cabin down there," Mom said. "It's very rustic—very back to basics. He's going to let us spend Christmas there."

"What's 'rustic'?" Joe said.

"I think we're talking no TV, no phone, no VCR," Art said. He cocked an eyebrow at Mom. "Am I right?"

"Absolutely," Mom said. "From what I understand, it has heat and hot water, but that's it for amenities."

"I don't even know what amenities are," Joe mumbled. "But I don't think I can make it without 'em."

"You'll live," Mom said. "When we arrive, we're going to decorate the cabin for Christmas with whatever we can find in the surrounding woods."

"That sounds cool!" Lily said hopefully. "Will we be able to chop down a tree? You know, to put the presents under?"

"No tree chopping," Dad said. "And no presents—at least, not any store-bought gifts."

Lily felt her neck snap as she brought her head as upright as it would go. Across from her, Joe and Art were doing the same thing. If she hadn't been in shock, she would have thought the three of them must look like E.T.'s triplet siblings.

"There *will* be presents," Mom said, "but they have to be home-made or non-tangible."

Joe opened his mouth. Art leaned toward him and said, "That means it can be something you can't hold in your hand. Like you taking all my chores for next year."

"That's the idea," Dad said, nodding his head approvingly.

"Fat chance!" Joe said to Art.

Once again, Mom and Dad looked at each other, and suddenly Lily saw what it was they were trying to change. But they were doing it all wrong as far as she was concerned. If they grounded Art and Joe for about six months, they'd get the message sooner. Well, maybe it would take nine months for Joe.

"Pack warm, rugged clothes," Mom said. She looked at Lily. "This isn't going to be a glamour gig."

"Ya think?" Art said with a snicker.

Joe didn't say anything. He appeared to be sunken down too far into his gloom.

"In addition to clothes and toilet articles—"

"We gotta take our own toilet paper?" Joe said.

"She means your toothbrush, moron!" Lily said. Then she wanted to bite her tongue off. *Okay, so I might need to be grounded too*, she thought. *Maybe for a week.*

"In addition to the basics," Mom went on as if nobody had said anything, "you are required to bring three items and only three items, and they are to be as follows—"

"Write this down, Lily," Art said.

Lily nodded and grabbed the pad and pen, which were never far from where Dad was.

"You must bring one book—and only one—one game—and only one—and one food treat—"

"And only one," Lily, Art, and Joe said in unison.

"That's it."

Mom gave her ponytail a shake and looked at Dad. He nodded at her and refolded his hands.

"That's it?" Joe said. "That's gonna be Christmas?"

"Your mother and I are each going to bring the three items as well," Dad said.

"Goodie," Joe said. "That'll make it just—"

Art clapped his hand over Joe's mouth. Lily glared at the kid. Isn't it bad enough, Joe, without you insulting Dad? He's liable to make it worse!

Though she was sure it couldn't get much worse.

"I'm taking the van in this morning to have the heater worked on," Dad said. "This afternoon I want you three to clean it out and get it all spruced up inside for the trip."

Okay—so it *could* get worse.

"This is gonna be like the worst Christmas on the planet," Joe said late that afternoon as each of the Robbins kids took a seat in the van, garbage bag in hand. "Can't we call the authorities or somethin' and complain?"

Lily brought her head up from between the front and second seats and smacked a stray curly tendril off her forehead with annoyance. "What authorities?" she said.

"The child abuse people!" Joe said. "I don't think parents are allowed to treat kids like this!"

"Look, guys," Art said from the front seat. "Mom and Dad are just going through some kind of middle-aged weirdness phase. They'll get over it."

"In the next five days?" Lily said. "I don't think so. I think—"

"Don't tell us what you think, okay?" Joe said. "Last time you told us what to do, we did it! And Mom and Dad took away Christmas!"

"Like you weren't gonna make a Christmas list on your own," Art said. "Did she have to twist your arm?"

"It was her idea," Joe said stubbornly. Then he ducked behind the seat and continued muttering into his trash bag. "I was really countin' on a scooter."

Yeah, well, don't feel like somebody special, Lily thought as she pried a half-eaten Jolly Rancher off the floor mat. *I not only was counting on camping equipment—I already told all the Girlz I was getting it. And I told Reni I'd call her and read my list to her. Huh—there is no list! I'm gonna look like an idiot!*

When the next thought hit, Lily put her head down on the seat and felt herself going red-hot in the face. *And I know I made Kresha and Zooey feel like they're poor or something after I bragged about what I was getting. Dude—even Kresha's gonna get more than me now!*

"Hey!" Joe said suddenly. "The UPS truck's comin' down the street!"

Lily crawled up onto the seat and stretched her neck to see out the back window where Joe had his face glued.

"I betcha he's bringin' stuff from Mudda," Joe said. "Good old Mudda—she'll come through with some loot."

"Jo-oe!" Lily said. But she found herself hoping their grandmother *had* come through as the familiar brown truck headed toward them. She sagged against the seat when it passed.

Yikes, she thought. *All my presents are gonna be like the ones Kresha and Zooey gave me.*

That evening Lily packed, still venting as she shoved sweatshirts and boots and thermal underwear into her bag. Mom had said they'd be roughing it. That was what the survival people at church had said, too, but this didn't feel like she'd expected to feel when she was getting ready to go out and be Outdoor Woman.

And it wasn't just the fact that there was no new sleeping bag waiting to be packed and no new hiking boots to put on. She was going to be stuck in a cabin with Art and Joe instead of roaming the wild outdoors with her Girlz. She was going to have to eat whatever gross, disgusting treat Joe was bringing along instead of fishing for trout and toasting marshmallows over an open fire. And she was going to be expected to learn a lesson she'd already figured out the minute Mom and Dad told them about this trip—don't be greedy and don't be mean to your brothers. She'd much rather be surviving in the wild with those professionals who were going to show them what it was like for Jesus and the disciples when they were traveling around. Now *that* was a lesson she wasn't going to be able to pick up in the first thirty seconds the way she had this time.

Lily reached inside her bag to stuff her *Talking to God* journal in and felt something move. She squealed and tumbled backward. Otto wriggled out of the bag and shook himself off.

"This is the worst part of *all*!" Lily said to him. "I can't even bring *you*!"

She'd begged all through dinner to be allowed to take him on the trip, but Mom and Dad wouldn't budge. Otto was going across the street to the neighbors, and that was that.

"If I'm gonna have any Christmas at all, I'm gonna have to make it for myself," she told him as he curled his wiry form up in her lap.

She glanced at the three items she'd chosen that she still needed to put in her bag.

One book: the survival book she'd checked out of the library that afternoon. At least she could read it and *pretend* she was being Outdoor Woman.

One game: Barbie Monopoly. Her brothers hated it, but Joe was going to be so bored without TV, and Art was going to be going crazy without the telephone. They'd have no choice but to play it with her.

One treat: a package of red licorice. She was the only one in the family who liked it, so it was a sure thing nobody else was going to bring any.

Lily sighed as she gathered Otto up to her face so he could slurp it.

"It doesn't look like much of a Christmas, Otto," she said. "Not much of a Christmas at all."

Chapter 3

Lily was teary-eyed the next morning as she climbed into the van after taking Otto across the street.

"You are *way* too attached to that dog," Art said.

"Yeah, man," Joe said, "that's weird."

Lily opened her mouth to sling out a comeback, but she caught Mom's eye and stopped herself. It was obvious to Lily that it was going to be up to her—and her alone—to convince Mom and Dad that the kids had learned the necessary lesson. There were still four days left until Christmas. That was enough time to shop—if she could just get Art and Joe to *shut up!*

Besides, she thought as she hunkered down in the van's second seat and tried not to be aware that Joe was sharing it with her, *it isn't just Otto I'm already homesick for. There's the Girlz—and the living room that didn't even get decorated at all—and the kitchen, where we don't even get to make cookies. 'Course, Joe always made stupid stuff with his frosting—Rudolf all bloody after he crashed with the sleigh—stuff like that. Maybe I won't miss that part.*

But everything else from checking the mailbox every day for cards to staying up late helping Mom wrap presents—she missed it all.

"And what about church?" she said out loud.

"What about it?" Art said from the backseat, which he had claimed all for himself, since he was the oldest. His voice was testy. Probably, Lily decided, because Mom and Dad wouldn't let him bring his portable CD player and earphones. She'd heard him mutter as they were leaving the house that this must be what it was like to go through drug withdrawal.

"We're gonna miss the Christmas Eve service," Lily said. "That's my favorite."

"Not to worry, Lilliputian," Dad said, looking at her in the rearview mirror. "We're going to have our own worship service. You can all help plan it."

"Goodie," Joe said under his breath.

Art grunted.

Lily sighed.

Mom looked over at Dad. "Hon," she said to him, "I think we have a long way to go."

Lily was pretty sure she wasn't talking about the distance to North Carolina.

"Can we at least turn the radio on?" Art said.

"Why don't we sing some carols instead?" Dad said. "Take turns picking."

Joe started singing immediately, "We three kings of Orient are, trying to smoke a rubber cigar. It was loaded. It exploded." He took a breath and changed tunes. "Si-ilent night."

"Man, that is *so* old," Art said.

"You got somethin' better?" Joe said.

"Jingle bells—Batman smells—Robin laid an egg—"

"Oh, *do* shut up!" Lily said.

"How about *Joy to the World*?" Dad said.

"Joy to the world!" Joe sang, "the school burnt down! And all the teachers too. Except for the principal. They tied him to the flagpole— and listened to him scream. And listened to him scream—"

"Never mind," Mom said. She looked at Dad again. "Do you have any more good ideas?"

Lily snapped around in her seat and glared at Art and then at Joe.

"What?" Art said innocently.

"You two are *not* helping!" Lily said between clenched teeth.

"You're not the boss of me, you know," Joe said.

"What is it we're supposed to be doing to *help*?" Art said.

"Oh, never mind!"

"Good!"

"Loser!"

"Major loser!"

"Wimp—"

The bickering continued along those lines on and off all morning until Art finally dozed off in the backseat, his smelly feet propped up close to Lily's nose, and Joe amused himself by singing "There Was an Old Lady Who Swallowed a Fly" under his breath. Lily sat in sullen silence and watched Delaware and Maryland go by. They both looked pretty much alike in their gray slush and their light-pole decorations. Every plastic lit-up angel seemed to be saying, "Nee-ner, nee-ner, nee-ner—you get a rotten Christmas!" Lily was almost glad when Art woke up and started complaining that he was hungry. It blocked out the angels.

"When are we stopping for lunch?" Art said.

"*Where* are we stopping?" Joe said.

"I vote for Wendy's," Art said. "I want chili."

"Nah—they don't have any cool toys right now," Joe said. "I want McDonald's."

"Not that you're getting any toys anyway," Lily said. She stole a look up at the front seat to see if Mom and Dad were hearing that she, at least, had caught on. "I think Taco Bell."

"No, man!" Joe said. "You'll be burping burritos all afternoon back here!"

"Don't worry about it, Joe," Mom said. "We already have a lunch plan, and it doesn't include any of the above."

"Pizza?" Art said weakly.

Mom shook her head and dug into her purse as Dad pulled the van into the parking lot of a Bi-Lo grocery store.

"Huh?" Joe said.

Mom turned to them with several slips of paper she'd just extracted from her purse. She held them in her cupped hands and said, "Pick one."

"What are they?" Joe said.

"They're cigarette papers," Art said. "We're all gonna light up."

"Really?" Joe said to Mom.

Lily groaned.

"Why don't you pick one and read it, and then you'll know what it is," Mom said.

Lily guessed that was her high school teacher voice. It was a voice her volleyball team didn't mess around with, and neither did any of the Robbins kids. Art climbed halfway over the seat to get his piece of paper, and Joe snatched one up like he expected Mom to bite his hand off if he didn't do it fast enough. Lily took one of the three that was left.

Cheese, it said.

She looked up at Mom with a question already on her lips, but Mom plunked four dollar bills into her hand and said, "Get the item on your paper with this money and be back here in fifteen minutes. We're going to have a picnic lunch, and you each have part of the menu."

"Nice day for it," Art said as he looked up at the gray sky that was smeared like paste over the shopping center. "You sure know how to pick 'em."

"Thank you, son," Mom said. "You now have fourteen minutes. You better get it moving."

It took Lily only five minutes to find the kind of cheese you squirted out of a can, but it took her another seven to decide whether she could bear to eat it without the Girlz. They always ate this kind at Girlz Only meetings and just looking at it made her homesick for them. It also made her think of decorating cookies with the frosting that came in a tube.

Lily was the last one to climb into the van just as it was starting to snow.

"Snow?" Art said. "This is Virginia. It doesn't *snow* in the South."

"It's not even going to stick." Dad said. He rubbed his palms together. "Let's see what's to eat, huh? Who had the bread assignment?"

The kids all looked blankly at each other.

Art gave Joe a poke. "Did you have it, Squirt? B-R-E-A-D."

"Shut up!"

"You had it," Mom said to Dad.

"Oh." Dad grinned as if he were having the time of his life and pulled five rolls out of his bag. "Voilà!" he said.

"We really gotta get him out of the house more often," Art murmured to Lily.

"I'm next," Mom said. "I had the meat assignment, so I picked up some nice deli turkey."

"Nice work, dear," Dad said to her.

"Thanks. You, too, hon," Mom said back.

"No fair," Joe said. "I saw you two talkin' in there."

"Who said we weren't supposed to talk?" Mom said. "I'd have shown any of you what I was getting if you'd asked." She scanned the three faces. "Who had cheese?"

"Me," Lily said. She pulled one can of cheese halfway out of her bag.

"Oh, yummy," Art said. "Won't that be divine with turkey on a kaiser roll?"

"I hope somebody got condiments," Dad said. "I think we definitely at least need some mustard."

"Oh," Joe said. "Is that what condiments are?" He turned his bag over and dumped out a jar of peanut butter.

"Excuse me while I throw up," Lily said.

"So I guess you had the beverage," Mom said to Art. "What are we washing this gastronomical disaster down with?"

"Good old Mountain Dew!" Art said as he pulled a giant green bottle from his bag. "It was on sale."

"Wonderful," Mom said to Dad. "We're going to be peeling them off the ceiling."

"Okay, let the grazing begin!" Dad said.

Lily could feel one side of her upper lip curling. "This is gonna be disgusting," she said. "How are we supposed to eat peanut butter and turkey together? Gross me out and make me icky!"

"I'm gonna pass on the squeeze cheese on a bun, thank you very much," Art said. "You shoulda gotten some Swiss from the deli department."

"Oh, and Mountain Dew was a great choice," Lily said. "Like that goes with everything."

"Now what would have made this whole lunch thing better?" Dad said as he carefully folded a piece of turkey onto his roll and then looked dubiously at Lily's can of cheese.

"If Joe would have asked somebody what a condiment was," Lily said.

"Or if you woulda thought of somebody but yourself!" Joe shot back. "And you know what, Dad? I mean, no offense, but I only like peanut butter on white bread. Just plain old white bread."

"All right," Dad said, his voice still calm. "So we've determined that two things are going to be required if we're all going to enjoy this vacation together."

One—we lose Art, Lily thought, *and two, we lose Joe.*

But she squeezed out a finger full of cheese and said nothing.

"Communication," Dad said. "And consideration." He took the bottle of Mountain Dew Mom handed him as if she'd just given him a dirty diaper to hang onto. "I don't think there was much of that going on while you were shopping."

"Right you are, Dad!" Art said. "I think we learned that lesson, huh guys?"

Lily nodded enthusiastically. At least Art was finally getting a clue.

"I suggest we all celebrate over a bowl of chili," Art went on. "Or—no—I'm even willing to go for a Quarter Pounder with cheese."

"Nice try," Dad said. "Seconds on squeeze cheese, anyone?"

"Barf," Joe said, and he scooped two more fingers of peanut butter out of the jar.

"Come on, Mom," Art said. "I know you have food stashed in here someplace. Or were we planning to kill squirrels to eat when we got to the cabin?"

"Watch your tone," Dad said, his tone a warning.

"We're all going to go grocery shopping together when we get closer," Mom said. She arched her eyebrows. "I guess I learned who *not* to send down the beverage aisle."

It was snowing harder by the time the kids had griped their way through lunch and Dad got the van under way again. The faster the windshield wipers slapped the snow out of the way, the faster it fell. Lily wished there were wipers on the side windows, because by mid-afternoon she could barely see anything. Snow was gathering at the bottom and hardening there, just like the spray-on kind they'd used at home on years when there wasn't a white Christmas.

Dad hunched over the steering wheel as the traffic slowed to a crawl, and now and then he ran his hand across the back of his neck. The only other time Lily had seen him do that was when he was filling out an income tax form. Art leaned restlessly on the back of Lily's seat.

"How come everybody's drivin' so slow?" he said. "Buncha wimps."

"They don't have snow tires like we do," Mom said. Her mouth twitched. "We're in the South."

"So they oughta pull off the road," Art said. "Look at that—they don't even know how to drive in this stuff!"

The van lurched as Dad pumped the brakes to avoid hitting the little red Honda Civic that had just pulled in front of them—and then swerved back over to its own lane.

"What the devil!" Art said.

"He isn't doing it on purpose," Dad said. "He's sliding on the ice."

"Like I said, he needs to get off the road."

"Maybe *we* should get off the road," Mom said. She pulled her ponytail tight and crossed her arms. "We aren't on a schedule. Why don't we stop at a motel for the night?"

"Yes!" Joe, Art, and Lily said in unison.

At least we agree on something, Lily thought.

All three of them watched Dad, biting back the coaxing Lily was sure the boys wanted to do as much as she did. But Dad just rubbed the back of his neck again and said, "It's bound to let up here pretty quick. We'll keep going."

"Has anybody bothered to listen to a weather report?" Art said.

Mom threw him a dagger look.

"Just asking," Art said.

A silence fell in the car that was thicker than the snow and just as cold. Lily tried to concentrate on a warm hotel room with a huge bathtub—and maybe room service. She'd never *had* room service, but she'd seen it in movies. They always served it with those silver things covering the plates.

No—I'm Outdoor Woman, she reminded herself. *Maybe we'll have to drive all night. That would be kind of like survival.*

Maybe there would be some hints in her survival book. She leaned over to dig through her backpack. The van lurched again, pitching her headfirst toward the floor, and she heard Mom yell, "Watch him! He's coming over!"

"Dude, man—run us off the road, why don't you?" Art said.

Before Lily could pull her head up to see what was going on, the van lurched again, and then it seemed to float—around in circles.

"Hang on!" she heard Dad cry out.

Lily groped for a handhold, and her hands landed on something thin that gave under her fingers as she latched on. The van stopped spinning and slammed to an abrupt halt. Icy snow sprayed the window above Lily, and then everything was quiet and still.

Lily held on tight and squeezed her eyes shut and waited for something to hurt.

Chapter 4

Is everybody all right?" Dad said.

"No!" Joe said. "Lily's holding onto my leg, and she's cutting off my circulation!"

"Stop the bickering for two seconds!" Mom snapped. "Is everyone okay?"

One by one the kids checked in, all in quivery voices, even Art, though he recovered first.

"What happened to the Honda Civic?" he said as he scrubbed at the window to look out. "He runs us off the road and then takes off—dude!" He turned to the rest of them, his eyes wide. "We are stuck, man—I mean, totally stuck."

"Cool!" Joe said, and went after his window with the side of his fist.

"I'm going to go out and assess the situation," Dad said, pulling on his gloves. "Everybody just sit tight."

"You don't want me to go with you, Dad?" Art said.

"No. Stay here."

The door slammed, and Art leaned over the seat, past Lily. "Mom, you oughta let me go out there. Dad's no good at this kinda stuff."

"You heard him," Mom said. "Just sit tight."

But she didn't look any more certain than Art did that Dad was going to have a clue what to do. Lily had heard Mom say a hundred times that their father was one of the most brilliant men she knew, but when it came to cars, she would trust her vehicle to Otto before she would let Dad lift the hood.

Lily crowded up to the window next to Joe and watched through a hole in the frost as Dad plowed through the snow, which was already up to his ankles and piling up more. He slipped down the small incline the van had dove into and shook his head. He couldn't have raised the hood if he'd tried, because the van was wedged head-on into a ditch that was quickly filling up with snow.

They all peered out through the fast-fogging windows as Dad made his way to the other side of the van and shook his head again. The wind was blowing so hard, he had trouble making his way back to the door and had to practically wrestle with it to get it closed as he climbed into the front seat. Snow blew in on icy air before he could finally slam it.

"My gosh," Mom said, "your eyebrows are already freezing. Let me turn this heater up."

"Up?" Art said. "First you gotta turn it *on*. It's not even blowing."

Mom turned the knob, but nothing happened.

"Oh, rats," Dad said. "They told me they'd fixed that thing."

"They may have," Mom said. "But it just took a heck of a jolt."

"Then it looks like we need a plan, group," Dad said. "Because we're not going to get this thing out of here without a wrecker."

"I could try to back it out, Dad," Art said. "I could drive and every-body else could push."

"It's not going to happen!" Dad said. "Now let's move on. We're going to have to figure out how to stay warm until help arrives."

"I'm cold already," Joe said.

"There are some blankets behind the backseat," Mom said. "Art, could you grab them? We have to try to keep our body temperatures up. We could be sitting here a while."

Art didn't lean over the seat but instead dug into his bag.

"Come on, man," Joe said. "I'm freezin'."

"Maybe not for long," Art said.

He pulled a small, black item out of the bag and held it up. Lily recognized it as Mom's cell phone.

"I know I wasn't supposed to bring this," he said. "But as long as we've got it, we can use it to call somebody to get us out of here."

Mom and Dad gave Art identical long, hard looks. For two people who didn't even vaguely resemble each other, they could sure look alike at times.

Lily took the phone from Art and passed it up to her parents. She then gave him a hard look of her own.

"What were you thinking?" she whispered to him. And then she shook her head. Of course—he'd brought it so he could call Marsha. *This* was going to get them a lot closer to a real Christmas. Oh, brother.

Dad called the number for roadside assistance, which he found on the map, and told them the "situation," as he called it. Lily would have called it a disaster. It became more of one when the people told Dad they would get to the Robbins as soon as they could, but there were several other accidents they had to get to first because they involved injuries.

"The guy says this is far more snowfall than is normal for this area," Dad said as he punched the "end" button on the phone—and handed it to Mom, not Art. "He says they just don't have enough snow removal equipment to handle all the calls they're getting."

"Are we gonna freeze to death?" Joe said.

"No, moron," Art said, and threw a blanket at him.

"Are we gonna starve to death?"

"Of course not," Mom said. Her mouth twitched a little. "We have all those delicious leftovers from lunch."

There was a unanimous groan.

"What about my treat I brought?" Joe said. "Can I eat that now?"

"Absolutely," Mom said. She reached back and put her hand on Joe's arm as he lunged for his backpack. "As long as you share it with everybody."

"He wants to!" Lily said, baring her teeth in a threatening smile at Joe. "He totally does—don'tcha, Joe?"

Joe gave her his you-are-Looney-Tunes-girl look and said to Mom, "Sure. If anybody wants any."

That made Lily suspicious, and she watched closely as he produced his treat. It was Sour Patch Kids—a candy so gross they *gave* it away at the movie theater when you bought a large popcorn and a drink.

"Some?" Joe said, offering the opened box to Art.

"No, thanks," Art said. "I'm tryin' to quit."

Everybody else shook their heads before Joe even had a chance to ask again. He munched happily as they huddled in their blankets and listened to their stomachs growl.

At least it's keeping him quiet, Lily thought. *Every time he opens his mouth he makes things worse. We're gonna end up living in that cabin pretty soon!*

It wasn't long before darkness descended on the van, which made it seem all the more like they were being buried in snow.

"Is there enough air in here for all of us to breathe?" Lily said.

"Oh, brother," Joe said. Then he narrowed his eyes at Dad and said, "Is there?"

"Yes, we're going to be fine," Dad said. "Why don't you try to get some sleep?"

Joe chose instead to pick up where he left off with the old lady swallowing the fly song—at least he sang quietly to himself. Lily looked at the window, through which she could see only a steady fall of thick, heavy flakes. It looked like someone in heaven was dumping them out of buckets.

God, she prayed miserably, *could you please stop this, just long enough for us to get out of here? I'll even go to the cabin without any more whining—I promise. But it's cold—and we're hungry—and I'm sorry I've been such a pill about Christmas. I really am. And if there's something you want me to do to help—*

She jerked her head away from the window and looked down at her bag. Of course! The survival book. There had to be something in there about staying warm and not getting frostbite and stuff.

Lily leaned forward and rested her chin on the back of Mom's seat.

"Could I use the flashlight that's in the glove compartment?" she said.

"What do you need it for?" Mom said. "Did you lose something back there?"

"No—I just want to read."

Mom shook her head. "We need to save the batteries, Lil," she said. "We don't know how long this night might be or whether we'll need a light at some point."

"But I want to read my survival book—"

"Your mother said no," Dad said—in a voice so unusually sharp it pushed Lily right back into her seat.

"Busted," Joe said under his breath.

"The only way any of you are going to survive this night," Mom said, glancing at Dad, "is to lay low. I suggest a long nap."

Art was already half-snoring in the back. Lily pulled her blanket around her and curled up on her side of the seat, being careful not to trespass over the invisible line Joe kept under constant surveillance. She used the armrest for a pillow and finally dozed off about the time Joe got to the old lady swallowing a cow.

When she woke up, he was snuggled up against her, his head nestled on her thigh. *That* grossed her out—and made her icky—but the sound of Dad's voice in the front seat diverted her attention. He obviously wasn't talking to Mom, because her head was lolled against the window on the passenger side.

"It isn't an emergency yet," Lily heard Dad say in a stone-serious voice, "but it's definitely urgent. We have no heat, no food to speak of, and we have three children—"

There was a pause. Lily sat up, letting Joe's head roll to the seat, and leaned up to watch Dad. He had the cell phone pressed hard against his ear.

"That would be wonderful," he said. "You have our location?" Another pause. "Right. We'll see you within the hour."

He ended the call and gave Mom a gentle nudge.

"Jo—" he said. "Wake up, hon. We've got help coming."

Mom sat up sleepily, and Lily gave Joe and Art each a poke. She'd had to wake them up before—it was pointless to waste gentle nudges on them.

"What's up?" Mom said.

"There's a volunteer rescue squad coming to get us," Dad said. "They're going to take us to a shelter where we can stay until somebody can get the van out and it's safe to drive on."

"Thank the Lord," Mom said. She stroked Dad's arm.

"Can I go back to sleep 'til they get here?" Joe said.

"Yeah," Art said, and shoved Joe's head back into Lily's lap.

Lily was so happy about the news that she didn't even cringe.

A rescue squad! she thought. *Thank you, God! You are the best!*

She would have prayed more, but as she hugged her blanket around her, all she could think about was a hot bath and a warm hotel room and the possibility of pizza.

Chapter 5

Lily was so excited by the time help arrived that she was feeling warmer. As a large, Jeep-like vehicle with oversized tires drove up, it was all she could do not to ask her mom, "Do you think we could get extra pepperoni?"

Dad wound his window down and put his hand out to clasp the hand and arm of a red-faced man who seemed to be lost somewhere in his snowsuit.

"I have never been so glad to see somebody!" Dad said. "God bless you, sir."

"Mah pleasure," said the man in an accent like none Lily had ever heard. She was used to crisp New Jersey dialect and Kresha's Croatian-flavored talk. This sounded like syrup coming out of the man's mouth.

"How many of ya'll are in there?" he said. "Five?"

"He talks cool," Joe whispered.

"I think I can get everybody in, long as you don't have too much to bring along."

"He doesn't have to worry about that," Art muttered.

They all grabbed their bags and blankets and steeled themselves for the blast that was going to happen when they slid open the door. But Lily was smiling. God had answered her prayer, and it was going to be okay now. Just to be on the safe side, though, Lily decided she was going to be the Consideration Queen from now on.

They piled into the big-wheeled Jeep and held their bags on their laps as they squished together. The man squeezed himself behind the wheel and turned up the heater.

"Yes!" Art said.

"You have no idea how good that feels," Mom said to the man. "I didn't catch your name."

"I guess you're going to need to know that, now, aren't you?" he said. "Name's Sandy. Sandy Claws."

There was a brief silence in the Jeep, until Joe said, "Nuh-uh!"

"Had you goin' there for a minute, though, didn't I?" the man said. "No—seriously, I'm Taylor Selby. Nice to meet ya'll."

They all introduced themselves, including Lily, though she didn't see what difference it made. They probably weren't going to ever see him again once he dropped them off at the hotel. Still, she'd vowed to be cooperative.

"So, Mr. Selby," she said. "What hotel are you taking us to?"

He glanced at her in the rearview mirror, his eyes barely visible in the small hole left for his face by the snowsuit hood.

"Sugar," he said, "I wish I *was* takin' ya'll to a hotel. We got some nice ones 'round heah—but darlin', I'm afraid they've been filled up since before noon." He laughed, though for the life of her Lily couldn't see a thing that was funny. "The first flake fell, and all those folks traveling up from the South grabbed those rooms so fast the desk clerks couldn't keep up with them."

Beside her, Lily could feel Art stiffening up. "Where *are* you taking us, then?" he said.

"They've got a real nice set-up over at the high school," Taylor Selby said. "It's warm, and there's plenty of room, and we've got some ladies fixing some food for everybody."

"Everybody?" Lily said.

"I reckon there's about fifty people over there by now. But don't you worry about it, Sugar—like I said, they got plenty of room in the gym. School's practically brand new, and it's got the biggest gymnasium in the county."

While he continued giving Mom and Dad statistics, Lily looked at Art to see if she was the only one who was finding this news pretty terrible. Art was looking a little green.

"A high school gym," he muttered. "My favorite place in the *whole* world. Right up there with the bottom of a dumpster."

Lily felt like ripping her cap off her head and chewing on it so she wouldn't scream, *No! No! No! I don't want to spend Christmas in a gym with strangers!*

Joe, on the other hand, was warming up to the idea.

"Hey, Mr. Taylor," he said. "Do they have basketballs there?"

"Mr. Selby, Joe," Mom said.

"That's all right, ma'am," Mr. Selby said. "Yes, my man, they have basketballs, soccer balls, baseballs—you name it."

Joe was practically holding his breath. "Can we use 'em?"

"You betcha. Couple hours ago when I was in there, a whole raft of men were shootin' baskets." He gave one of those nothing's-really-funny laughs again. "Probably easin' off the tension of a very rough day."

"I hear that," Dad said.

Lily and Art looked at each other. She knew he was thinking the same thing she was thinking—if Dad started playing basketball, they would know he was going through some middle-aged weirdness phase.

There was no stifling Joe's excitement the rest of the way to the high school. He wanted to know what the basketball team's record was—whether the court was regulation—whether the coach would be stopping by.

"He's a freak," Art whispered to Lily.

Lily nodded, but she thought, *At least somebody's happy about this.* It was getting harder by the second to be the Queen of Consideration. *I know I've already asked you for a lot of stuff tonight, God,* she prayed, *but could you help me be a good sport about this? This wasn't exactly what I was expecting.*

When they arrived at Thomas Jefferson Senior High School, Mom gave the expected compliments, as if Mr. Selby had built the thing himself.

"Joe's going to be right at home here," Dad told him. "He practically lives in a gym anyway."

"Great," Art muttered. "What about the rest of us?"

The rest of them and Mom trudged toward the school through the snow, which was by now up to Lily's knees. She glanced back at Dad and Art, who were bringing up the rear. Even from just a few steps away, she could barely make out their faces through the storm. She shivered, more from a little fear than from the cold. She'd seen a lot of snowstorms while growing up in New Jersey, but she'd never hung out with one the way they were doing tonight. It made the whole world look lonely and empty. It matched the way she was suddenly feeling inside.

Lily plastered a smile on her face, though, and followed Mr. Selby through a door he had to bang on to get somebody to open.

"Good security," he said as he held it open and the Robbins all filed past him. "Don't go out unless you know somebody's standin' by to let you back in."

"I don't think any of us will be going outside," Dad said. "It's going to take us a while just to thaw out."

There were clumps of melting snow all along the hallway as they trailed down toward the gym. It looked like the foot leavings of more than fifty people to Lily.

They had to pass the cafeteria en route, and Mr. Selby stopped to point it out to them.

"I know ya'll are hungry," he said. "So soon's you get settled, you can come back here and get you somethin' to eat, now that you know where it is."

Lily sniffed, but she didn't smell anything except the faint odor of baloney and too-ripe bananas, the usual aromas of a school cafeteria. Nobody seemed to be cooking anything.

She peeked in as they passed. There was an assembly line of ladies at a long table, putting together stacks of peanut butter and jelly sandwiches. It was *so* not pizza, Lily's stomach turned.

"Great," Art muttered to her. "All we need now is a little squeeze cheese and we're set."

Lily gave him a stiff smile and walked on.

Mr. Selby hadn't been kidding when he said the gym was big. It was a cavern of hardwood flooring and enormous foldout bleachers and cream-white cinder block walls emblazoned with banners that said, "GO PATRIOTS" and "ALL THE WAY TO STATE!" in red and blue letters. It didn't look at all like Christmas.

There were overhead lights on in the gym, but they'd been dimmed, apparently so people could try to get some rest. Little knots of weary-looking people were spreading blankets out in various places on the floor, but Lily didn't see how anybody was going to be able to sleep. There was a little kid howling. Several women were barking out orders to husbands who didn't seem to be following them because they were shouting into cell phones, their hair flattened from a whole day spent under knit caps.

"Pick yourself a spot," Mr. Selby said cheerily. "It's filling up fast."

Mom turned to him and took both of his hands between hers. "God bless you," she said. "You were our angel tonight."

"Okay—she's definitely going over the edge," Art said to Lily as they followed Dad and Joe across the gym floor. "Have you ever heard her talk about angels before?"

Joe and Dad—well, actually, Joe—selected a spot right under the basketball hoop.

"He said there can't be anymore playin' tonight because people are tryin' to sleep," Joe said. "But I want first dibs on it tomorrow." He looked at Art.

"Don't even think about it," Art said. "I'm not playin' with you, pal. I play the saxophone, the guitar, and the piano. I do *not* play sports. Got it?"

"You just hate it that I always beat you," Joe said, as cheery as Mr. Taylor or Selby or whatever his name was. Lily wondered sourly why he couldn't just have a regular name like normal people.

"I'll shoot some hoops with you tomorrow, Joe," Dad said, ruffling Joe's hair.

Lily stared. So did Art.

"You will?" Joe said. "No offense, Dad—but, I mean—do you know how? Have you ever played before?"

Dad chuckled. "A few times. I had to pass a series of athletic tests before your mother would marry me."

"All right, Mom!" Joe said.

"He's kidding, right?" Lily said to Art when Dad and Joe had gone off to find the rest rooms.

"Yeah. But he's also losing it. He's gonna hurt himself—I'd put money on it."

Lily stopped shaking out her blanket and watched Dad disappear with her brother into the hallway. Dad might be weirding out a little, but he and Joe sure seemed happy.

I have to get happy too, she told herself firmly. *I am Outdoor Woman. I am the Queen of Consideration. I can do this.*

She folded her blanket into thirds so it would make a thicker pad and then pulled her survival book out of her bag. Using the bag for a pillow, she settled back to read. She tried not to miss Otto too much. About now, he would be curling up behind her knees—and growling at that little kid who was still howling just a few groups away. Joe had obviously missed *that* little detail when he was picking out a spot.

Lily found the chapter on sleeping arrangements and started reading. Two pages into it, she knew she was in trouble.

The book gave great suggestions about making a mattress out of pine needles, finding a place for it out of the wind, and making a lean-to out of a jacket and a pair of jeans.

This isn't gonna help! Lily thought as she flipped impatiently through the rest of the chapter. They had everything in there for sleeping in the snow, the jungle, the desert, and a tropical island—but there was nothing that told her how she was going to get through however-many nights on a hard wooden floor with somebody's kid screaming ten feet away.

There isn't a pine needle within a hundred yards, she thought. *And even if I could get to it, it would be under a bunch of soppy snow!* She sighed and started to toss the book aside—but she didn't. She'd promised God. She had to follow through.

Readjusting her fanny so that a different part of it would be flattened against the floor, she started back at the beginning of the book. The first chapter was on general guidelines. *That might help,* she muttered to herself.

The very first one said in bold letters, BE RESOURCEFUL.

Lily rolled over on her side and said, "Hey, Art. What does 'resourceful' mean?"

"What?" Art said. He turned over to face her and gave her a grumpy look. "You're as bad as Joe."

"I don't *think* so!"

Art smeared his face with his hand. "It means you can use what you have on hand to solve a problem—something like that. Dude! I'm on vacation. I don't wanna have to think."

"Thanks," Lily said. She had a lot of thinking to do herself. Sitting up on her pad, she carefully scanned the gym with her eyes. What was here that she could use for a bed?

A pile of rope? No, too lumpy.

That bunch of plastic flags? Nah—not thick enough.

Her eyes stopped on one wall, which appeared to be padded with blue rectangles.

Too bad I can't sleep on the wall, she thought. *Why would they pad the wall anyway?*

She couldn't answer that question—so she asked herself another one—what if the pads came down somehow? They'd be perfect.

Lily made her way across the floor, carefully skirting the other families, who were squirming restlessly to get comfortable. One older guy was even moaning.

It was dark near the padded wall, but it didn't take long for Lily to figure out that the pads were attached to the wall with black strips of tape.

Bummer, she thought. *I guess I could rip it down, but I don't want to get in trouble.*

It was too tempting to resist, though. She would just tear a piece back a little and see if it left a mark or anything.

Lily pulled gently, and there was a familiar ripping sound. Even as she jerked her hand back she knew what it was. Velcro!

She gave the pad a firm yank at the top, and it fell easily into her hands all the way to the bottom. She couldn't hold back a triumphant grin as she hurried back to Camp Robbins with it and let it fall to the floor beside Art. He rolled over and squinted at her.

"Hey," he said, "where'd you get the tumbling mat?"

51

"Is that what it is?" Lily said.

"Yeah."

"Well, now it's my bed."

"Where'd you get it?"

Lily pointed. Art scrambled to his feet, but not before several other people got to theirs and were headed for the wall. Joe came in just in time to get the last one. More than a few people were left standing there—matless.

"Hey," one guy called out, pointing to Art. He was one of the men who had been screaming into his cell phone earlier. "You got three!"

"One for me and one for each of my parents," Art said.

"Are your parents here?" the guy said.

"Yeah," Art said. "They went to the cafeteria to get coffee."

"They'll be right back," Lily said, and smiled at the man. Art wasn't the fighting kind, but right now he looked like he wanted to slug the guy.

Lily curled up on her mat with her blanket over her. The kid had stopped crying. She couldn't feel the floor pressing against her hipbones. Ah—so that's what resourceful meant.

Thanks for the resourceful thing, God, she thought sleepily.

She was just about to close her eyes when she heard the moaning again. She looked over to where she'd seen the older man on the floor, grunting as he'd tried to find a comfortable position, but he wasn't there. The groaning was coming from the bottom row of the bleachers, which had been pulled out.

The man was there, and he looked even older than she'd imagined. He was so thin that he reminded Lily of a bicycle tire tube somebody had let the air out of. And he had thin hair to match, which he carefully smoothed with a bony hand before resting his head on his bunched-up coat. He was trying to make a bed out of the bleacher bench.

"That can't be any softer than the floor," Lily said.

"Maybe it's warmer," Art said—and then sagged in the middle and breathed hard. He was asleep already.

But the old man wasn't even close to sleep. His wrinkled face pulled into a wince as he tried to bring his legs up into that nice comfortable curl most people seemed to sleep in. Lily turned her head so she wouldn't have to see him. But the picture of him cringing at the feel of his own bones stayed in her mind and wouldn't let her rest.

Maybe I should've tried to get him a mat, Lily thought. *But I didn't even think about it. I'm sorry, God—*

"Huh," said a raspy voice above her.

Lily jerked around and stared.

A woman was standing over her, hands on hips, eyes glittering. There was an angry look on her face, and she was pointing it right down at Lily.

Chapter

6

The woman was wearing a black satin jacket with the name CHERISE embroidered on the front in hot pink thread. She didn't look like a Cherise to Lily. She looked like a Wicked Witch of the West. Lily came up to a sitting position before the woman could say, *I'll get you, my pretty!*

"Is something wrong?" Lily said.

"You dang right something's wrong!" Cherise said. "A young'un like you or him or him—" She slashed a long red fingernail in the direction of Joe and Art. "—ya'll can go to sleep just about anywhere. But an old man—" She jerked her almost-white blonde head toward the man on the bleachers. "Somebody like that needs a decent bed. He's the one that needs the mattress—" She kicked at Lily's mat with the pointy toe of a black patent leather boot and said, "not you!"

"I was just thinking about that," Lily said. She licked her lips, which had already gone dry. Having this Cherise person glaring down at her was like having the breath sucked out of her.

"Uh-huh," Cherise said. "Sure you were."

I was! Lily wanted to yell at her. But as tired and cranky and fed-up as she was, she held it back. This woman was likely to snatch her up by the hair or something.

So Lily got to her feet and bent down to pick up her mattress.

"You kids today," Cherise said. "I swear. If my own acted that self-ish, I'd smack her on the backside."

Yeah, well, I'm glad I'm not your kid, Lily thought.

She wasn't sure if she was supposed to wait for Cherise to dismiss her or whether the woman was going to stand there and watch her until she was certain Lily was going to turn the mat over to the old man. Since Cherise didn't move but remained, arms folded across the satin jacket, toe tapping the gym floor, Lily hiked the mat up under her arm and dragged it toward the bleachers where the old man fidgeted in his sleep.

"Don't look so happy about it," Cherise said behind her. "He'll think you actually *wanted* to be nice to him."

Lily had to bite down hard on her lower lip to keep from turning around and lashing out with whatever happened to zing out of her mouth. Keeping her neck stiff and her hands clenched around the tumbling mat, she made her way to the bleachers.

When she reached the old man, he startled awake as if a bus had just driven past and he'd meant to get on it. He looked around in confusion, though he was careful to smooth down his hair.

"Would you like something more comfortable to sleep on?" Lily said. "I have a mat you can use."

It seemed to take a minute for that to register with the old fella. But when it did, a smile broke over his face, cracking it into a web of lines. She could almost hear them crackling.

"Well, bless your heart," he said. "Isn't that nice? Now, honey, what are you going to sleep on?"

Lily shrugged as she laid the mat on the floor. "I'm young," she said. "I can sleep anywhere."

"Well, darlin', God bless you. That's just real nice."

He smiled again, so that his faded blue eyes almost disappeared into the cracks. Lily tried to smile back, but she was so tired.

"G'night," she said.

"Good night, honey. You have sweet dreams now."

I'll be lucky to have any dreams at all, Lily thought as she went back to Camp Robbins. *You can't dream when you're wide awake!*

And if she did have dreams, she figured they would be nightmares, because Cherise was still standing there watching her, as if she was convinced Lily would have second thoughts and go back and snatch the mat right out from under the old man.

"Huh," Cherise said when Lily got to her, and then turned on her high spiked heel and walked off.

Lily picked up her blanket and started folding.

"Man, who retired and put her in charge?" Art said from under his blanket.

"You heard all that?" Lily said.

"Heard it?" Art sat up, swept his blanket aside, and pointed to the bare floor under him. "Do you see a mat here? She kicked me in the rear end and woke me up and told me I was a poor excuse for a gentleman." His eyes turned to slits as he watched Cherise return to her campsite. "Good thing I am a gentleman, or I'd have told her to—"

"That's okay," Lily said. "I get your drift."

Art grunted and turned over. Lily lay down on her blanket pad and pulled her coat up around her. Her legs were hanging out, and the air in the gym was sort of chilly. And the floor was hard. And she was still hungry. And there wasn't a trace of Christmas anywhere.

But I don't even want Christmas now, God, she prayed. *I just want my own bed.*

She would have cried herself to sleep, but she was too tired.

When she woke up the next morning—after a night of waking up every time she turned over in hopes that she'd find that magic position—Lily felt like she had the flu. Everything hurt.

"I don't feel good," she said to Mom, who was already up and had her hair in its shiny ponytail and was folding up blankets. "I ache all over."

"Who doesn't?" Mom said.

"That old guy on the bleachers," Art said from underneath his blanket.

" You need some hot food," Mom said. "They've got oatmeal in the cafeteria."

"They got raisins for it too," Joe said.

To Lily's surprise, he was shiny-faced and in his tennis shoes and a clean sweatshirt. He was looking longingly up at the basketball hoop.

"I hate raisins," Art said. "Wake me up when they serve lunch."

"I'd get up if I were you," Mom said. "Unless you want to catch a rebound or two with your backside."

Art poked his head out and glared with his one open eye at Joe. "You're a freak," he said.

"But he's in a good mood," Mom said, her mouth twitching. "If that's what it takes, I wish you were *all* freaks."

"I'm in a good mood," Lily said. She jumped up from her blanket and shook out her hair. Queen of Consideration. Outdoor Woman. That's what she was.

"Which way to the cafeteria?" she said.

Mom pointed, and then she gave Art a nudge with the toe of her Nike. "I'm telling you, Art, here comes Joe with a basketball."

Lily laughed as she heard it bouncing in Art's direction, but she didn't stay to see how it was going to turn out. The mood Art was in, it could get ugly.

She couldn't blame Art, she decided as she followed a sleepy group of people down the hall. She was having a hard time staying in a good frame of mind herself, especially after last night's run-in with that Cherise woman. Even now, Lily glanced over her shoulder to make sure there wasn't a black satin jacket stalking her. All she saw was a teenage girl holding a little kid of about two by the hand. Lily couldn't tell whether it was a boy or a girl, since the kid was carrying a red blanket that pretty much covered up everything else. Lily remembered Joe dragging something like that around until he was about four and discovered baseball. The minute Mom had told him no self-respecting Phillie would be caught dead carrying a blanket into the outfield, he'd abandoned the thing—and not a moment too soon. It had always smelled like sour milk and stale Cheerios.

Lily smiled at the teenager, but she only half smiled back.

I know your pain, Lily wanted to say to her. *I hate it when I get stuck with my little brother.*

She was suddenly grateful that Joe knew how to entertain himself. He was currently the happiest person in their family.

There was no line in the cafeteria, and Lily realized why very quickly. The oatmeal the women were serving up looked like the stuff the contractors at her house had used to hang the new wallpaper. Her stomach was groaning for something, though, so she asked for just one scoop full and sat down with her bowl at an empty table.

Yuck. It hadn't been salted, and it stuck to the roof of her mouth.

Gross me out and make me icky.

The Queen of Consideration disappeared with the oatmeal as Lily dumped it into the trashcan.

I am so hungry! her insides cried. *I want pizza. I want Fruity Pebbles. I want . . . licorice. Yes!* Her treat that she was supposed to share with the family, who all hated the stuff.

Surely the rules had changed now that they were in a crisis situation. That was a term she'd read in the guidelines in her survival book, and it seemed to fit. This was definitely a crisis situation if there ever was one. If she didn't eat an entire package of red licorice, she was going to starve to death.

Lily's bag had been pushed to the wall to make room for the basketball game, which was now in progress. Under any other circumstances, she would have stood there for a few minutes, gaping at her father, who was jumping around on the court, waving his arms while Joe neatly evaded him and landed a shot.

Joe guessed right, she thought, *Dad doesn't know how to play basketball.*

But Lily didn't linger. The licorice was calling to her.

She dug it out, narrowly escaping being grazed by the ball when it went out of bounds, and scoped out the gym for a quiet place to enjoy her stash. On the bottom row of the bleachers on the side where nobody was camped—yet—looked like her best bet. Best not to *look* as if she were hiding.

Lily tucked the licorice into the pocket of her hooded sweatshirt, went to the bleachers, sat down, and tucked her hair into the hood. The red hair was always like a loudspeaker that blared out, "Look at me! Look at me!"

Finally she pulled out the first piece of shiny red rope and lifted it to her lips. The very smell of it made her want to cry with relief.

"What you got?" said a small voice.

Lily looked up. There was a kid standing in front of her. And not just one kid—several kids. All with bed-head hair and mouths hanging open and eyes sad. Eyes completely Christmasless.

"Licorice," Lily said.

The little boy moved in closer. All five of them did, until she could feel their hot little breath on her hands.

"What's licorice?" he said.

"It's candy," Lily said. "But you probably wouldn't like it."

She wanted desperately to take a bite, but it was impossible with ten longing eyes watching her every move.

"Why wouldn't I like it?" the little boy said.

"Because," Lily said. It was the reason Art had always used on her. It didn't work with this kid either.

"Because why?"

"Because—you have to acquire a taste for it."

"What's ac—what's that mean?"

"It means, it's a grown-up taste, and you have to get used to it."

"Can I try it?"

The little girl beside him didn't wait for an answer. She seemed to be as annoyed with all these questions as Lily was and snatched the rope right out of her hand. Before Lily could grab it back, half of it had disappeared into her mouth.

"Hey, give me some!" the little boy cried, along with a chorus of back-up wailers.

The little girl thrust the remaining two inches of licorice at him, but he made a yuck face.

"It's got your cooties on it!" he said.

"Oh, for Pete's sake," Lily said. "Here—take your own."

The little boy took the one Lily pulled out of her pocket and handed to him. The other three kids looked at her expectantly.

"I suppose everybody wants a piece," Lily said.

There were only four left, which meant only one for her. Her stomach moaned in protest.

"Okay—you guys are little so you can share one piece," she said.

But she didn't even get the piece bent to break it before two of the kids were crying.

"I want my own!" the little boy said. "Eric got his own! I want my own!'

"I want mine own too," the little girl said.

Lily sighed from her very toes and handed them each a whole piece. They magically stopped crying—they even smiled and said thank you—and then took off at a dead run in case she should change her mind.

There was still one little one standing in front of her, and for the first time, Lily saw that it was the one the teenage girl had been taking to the cafeteria. She didn't have the blanket with her right now, so it was obvious she was a girl. She had dark hair that fringed her forehead in wisps and eyes so big they seemed to take up half her face. It was hard to focus on that, however, because a stream of green gunk was oozing out of each nostril, headed for her mouth. Her upper lip was already crusted with something dried green. Lily definitely wasn't going to *share* a stick with this kid.

"You're not gonna like it," Lily said to her. "And it won't be good for your cold—"

"I like dat—dat mine!" the little girl said, and she took the last piece of licorice right out of Lily's pocket.

"Hey!" Lily said. "You little thief!"

The little girl didn't seem offended—or scared. She sat down on the floor and took a large bite out of the rope she had to hold with two hands. She bit it into two pieces, which delighted her to no end, then gurgled through the green stuff that was coming out of her nose, looked up at Lily, and said, "I like dat!"

She proceeded to take a bite out of each one and chew juicily. Red stuff bubbled from her mouth.

Oh, well, Lily thought. *As least now she has Christmas colors.*

"What on earth do you have?" a familiar voice demanded from across the gym.

There was no need to look up. It was Cherise, and she was coming Lily's way. Lily looked around for an escape route, but Cherise seemed to have eyes only for the little girl, who was now shoving licorice into her little bow of a mouth as fast as she could get it in there.

"What is that—is that *candy*?" Cherise said.

She bore down on the little girl exactly the way she'd stood over Lily the night before. The baby's eyes widened, but as she looked up at Cherise she said, mouth completely full, "I like dat. Dat mine."

"Huh!" Cherise said, and she picked her up, licorice, snot, and all. *Then* she looked at Lily. "Thank you for loadin' her up with sugar without asking," she said. The sarcasm was dripping worse than the little girl's nose. "I'll be bringing her to *you* when it's naptime, and *you* can put her to sleep."

"Okay," Lily said.

Cherise ignored her and started to walk away. But she took only two steps before she turned around and plunked the one now-gooey piece of licorice the little girl hadn't managed to consume on the bench next to Lily. Then without a word, she clicked away in her high-heeled boots.

Lily looked down at the licorice until it blurred in her tears.

Chapter 7

Lily smeared off the tears that escaped down onto her cheeks and stood up to head for the cafeteria. Her stomach was so empty it was aching. There didn't seem to be any choice but to give that oatmeal a second chance.

"Hey," somebody said.

Lily turned around. It was the teenage girl, the one who'd been in charge of the licorice snatcher earlier in the morning. She was taller than Lily and was probably at least four years older. She had an I-grew-up-too-fast look about her with her dyed-mahogany hair in a very current style. It was short and combed close to her head in front but standing out in the back in spikes that reminded Lily of the flames coming out of a rocket in a cartoon.

"Hi," Lily said to her. "Sorry—I'm all out of licorice."

The girl smiled a little, and Lily noticed her two crooked front teeth and big, dark brown eyes, which were made up with shiny blue eye shadow about a half inch thick.

"I don't want any licorice," the girl said. "I just wanted to say thanks for being so nice to Angel."

"Who's Angel?" Lily said.

The girl turned and pointed to the little snot-nosed girl who was currently screaming because Cherise was wiping her face.

"Oh," Lily said. "She didn't really give me much choice—but that's okay—I mean, she's cute—and—it was nothing."

The girl looked amused, the way Mom did when Lily rattled on, but at least she didn't roll her eyes like a lot of people. It was enough to make Lily say, "Well, I'm Lily."

"Torie," the girl said. "It's short for Victoria, but nobody calls me that."

"Oh," Lily said. "I'd want to be called Victoria—that sounds so elegant. But, I mean, Torie's nice too."

"I don't do elegant," the girl said. She looked down at her hip-hugging jeans and clunky clogs.

"Oh, me either," Lily said. "I tried once, but it wasn't me. I'm more the outdoorsy type."

"I haven't figured out my type yet," Torie said.

"Well, let me see," Lily said. She stepped back a little from Torie and looked her over. She was thin and wiry, but she wasn't awkward looking. In fact, she looked like she could be a little scary, except when she smiled. Even then, though, Lily was pretty sure she could take care of herself.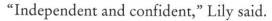

"Independent and confident," Lily said.

Torie let out a guffaw that echoed through the gym.

"Why is that funny?" Lily said.

"Oh, honey, if you only knew. But go on—tell me more about my type." She sat down on the bleacher bench and folded her arms. "I mean, you've known me for two minutes—you ought to be able to go into detail by now."

Lily liked the way Torie could say sarcastic things and not make it sound like she hated your guts. And she did seem genuinely interested in what Lily had to say, which wasn't happening all that frequently on this trip.

So Lily sat down next to her and thought about it. "I think you're smart but not school smart," she said. "Like if you got lost in a big city, you could find the right bus and not get mugged or anything."

"Go on," Torie said.

Lily did. She chatted on with Torie for what seemed like no more than a minute but must have been longer, because by the time Art walked up, Lily had found out that Torie and her mom—Cherise— and Angel were from Georgia. They were headed to New York to see some people. Torie, she now knew, was sixteen, the same age as Art, and wasn't doing too well in school. But she'd already risen to assistant manager at the Sunglass Hut where she worked. She wanted to become a fashion designer, and if she didn't find a Dr. Pepper within the next thirty minutes, somebody was going to get hurt. Lily was sure that in spite of the hard look she sometimes got around her eyes, Torie probably wouldn't hurt anybody.

Lily was about to ask her what it was like being Cherise's kid when Art walked up. He was now dressed in baggy blue jeans and an even baggier long-sleeved T-shirt so that he looked sort of loose-limbed. The way he had his hands stuffed into his pockets and his hair all moussed and styled-looking, Lily was pretty sure he was going for a casual look. She was also pretty sure it was all for Torie's benefit.

"Who's your friend?" Art said.

It took Lily a second to realize he was talking to her, because he was looking straight at Torie, who was looking straight back. Zooey had once informed Lily that that was called "checking each other out." Lily wished Art would check out somebody else. She and Torie were having a good time, and they didn't need him.

But she sighed and said, "Torie, this is my brother, Art."

"Nice to meet you," Art said. "I guess Lily's been telling you all the family dirt, huh?"

Lily already had her mouth open to protest, but Torie said, "No—actually, I've been doing most of the talking."

"You're kidding, right?"

"No. She's a good listener."

Make one rude comment about me, Art, and you are Dog Chow, Lily thought, teeth already clenched. Talking to Torie had made her feel better, but she was still hungry enough to eat somebody's leg off, and right now Art's was looking pretty appetizing.

"So what did I miss?" Art said.

"My entire life story," Torie said.

"Can I get the *Reader's Digest* version?"

"Only if you can find me a Dr. Pepper."

"They've got to have soda machines around here somewhere—I mean, come on, it's a high school."

"They have nothing but Pepsi," Torie said. "I *need* Dr. Pepper."

"I hear you. I just polished off the last of my Mountain Dew, and I'm already looking for another fix."

They grinned at each other. Lily waited for one of them to turn and include her in the smile loop, but nobody did. They were obviously still checking.

Man! Lily thought. *Everything I've tried to do to survive this place has backfired on me. I had to give up my bed—my food—now even my new friend. I think I need a different book.*

Lily started to sag, but she straightened her shoulders. Nope—she wasn't going to give up. She was a survivor, and that was all there was to it. It was time for a new approach.

"Hey, you guys," Lily said. "Why don't we go outside and mess around in the snow?"

Art looked at her as if she'd just grown an ear out of the center of her forehead. But Torie gave the biggest smile yet.

"Cool!" she said. "I've been wantin' to teach Angel how to make a snow angel. Ya'll ever done that?"

"That thing where you lie down in the snow and do your arms like this?" Art waved his arms up and down. "Yeah, I've done that."

Lily stared at him. If she had suggested it, he would currently be denying he'd ever heard of such a thing. But since it had been Torie, he was nodding his head and looking for all the world like he couldn't wait to throw himself down in the snow.

Even now, he gave Torie a nudge and said, "Get your stuff on. We'll meet you by the door."

Art Robbins, you are so lucky you said "we" and not just "I," Lily thought as she hurried to keep up with his long stride toward Camp Robbins for their coats. *Just don't you forget this was my idea!*

Dad was standing near their bags talking to Mr. Taylor—or was it Mr. Selby? Lily still couldn't keep it straight. Dad's hair was standing up in sweaty spikes, and his face was blotchy with heat. Yeah, it had definitely been a long time since *he'd* played basketball. Joe was nearby, dribbling and making hook shots, and Lily knew he was wishing someone would come along and challenge him.

"Hey, ya'll!" Mr. Selby said. "You enjoyin' our school? Did I tell you this was the biggest gymnasium in the county?"

"You did," Art said. As he bent down to get his coat out of his bag, he muttered to Lily, "Several times."

"Where you off to?" Dad said. He was eyeing the gloves Lily was hurriedly pulling on.

"We're gonna play in the snow," Lily said. "Torie wants to teach Angel how to make snow angels, and we'll probably—"

"She what?"

Lily groaned. It was Cherise. Did the woman wait around for chances to jump on her? Didn't she have anything else to do?

"Victoria!" Cherise shouted. She was so loud, everybody in the gym turned to look at her.

"Who's Victoria?" Art said to Lily.

Torie came up behind her, carrying Angel and tying a hat under the baby's chin.

"Yes, ma'am?" Torie said.

That surprised Lily. She had Torie pegged for the kind of daughter who answered, *"What?"* to a call like that.

"What were you thinkin'?" Cherise said. "No, you weren't thinkin'—that's your problem."

"Thinking about what?" Torie said. "Hold still, baby, let me get this tied."

"About taking this child out in the snow," Cherise said. "How were you planning to get her clothes dry when you came back in? Snow is *wet,* Torie. It doesn't just brush off like it does on the soap operas."

"Well, I—"

"Wipe her nose. Do you even *have* a tissue?"

"No, I left them over—"

"You see what I'm talking about when I say you have no sense of responsibility for that child?"

Lily wanted to peel back a floorboard and crawl under it. It was bad enough to get yelled at, but right here in front of strangers? Lily was ready to die, and she wasn't even the one under fire. She didn't look at Torie, just so she wouldn't embarrass her more.

Dad cleared his throat, and Cherise looked at him as if he'd just shown up.

"Excuse me, Mrs.—" Dad's eyebrows went up into question marks.

"Duncan," she said. "Cherise Duncan."

"Nice to meet you. I'm Paul Robbins. Mr. Selby here was just telling me that there's a lake on campus which has frozen over—"

Cherise glared at Torie. "Were you going to teach her to ice skate too?"

"We're goin' ice skating?" Joe said as he dribbled over to the group. "Anybody want to play hockey?"

"It isn't safe to walk on," Dad went on. "It's covered in snow, so it's hard to even see it until you're on top of it. That's my main concern about you going out there. I'm afraid somebody's going to go right through the ice before they even know they're on it."

"We don't want any accidents," Mr. Selby said. He looked a little sad for the kids as he put a hand on Joe's shoulder. "Too bad, too—I bet you're one good little hockey player."

As Joe went on to regale Mr. Selby with tales of his killer slap shot, Lily finally sneaked a look at Torie. She was whispering to Angel. As Lily watched, Torie tickled the little girl's tummy, and she giggled, blowing a bubble out of her nose.

"Look—you got a bubble!" Torie said.

"Go get a Kleenex!" Cherise said. "And get her out of those clothes before she fries."

"Or you could do it yourself, lady," Art whispered for Lily's bene-fit. "Torie's cool. Too bad she's gotta be her mom's full-time babysitter."

"Really," Lily said. But as Dad, Mr. Selby, and Cherise all moved away from them, she was already thinking about her next plan. They had to do *something* to pass the time or *nobody* was going to survive— especially Torie.

"Hey," Lily said suddenly. "I have an idea."

"Does it involve that chick in the black jacket?" Art said.

"No."

"That's half of it right there. Does it involve Torie?"

"Yeah."

"There's the other half. Let's hear it."

"What game did you bring?"

"Game?"

"You know—we were each supposed to bring a game to share with the family in the cabin."

"Oh." Art shrugged.

"Didn't you bring one?"

"Yeah, but it won't work. It's a computer game."

"How were you planning to play that with no computer?" Lily said.

"I figured Mom and Dad would have brought along the laptop, which they woulda let us use once they got over whatever it was they were trying to do."

"Aa-art!"

"You sure you guys don't wanna play some basketball?" Joe said, sidling up to them, ball on his hip as if it were attached to him. "I promise I'll go easy on ya."

"What game did you bring?" Lily said.

Joe dropped the ball and bounced it, giving it his full concentration.

"You know," Lily said. "The game Mom and Dad said to bring—"

"I know," Joe said. "I brought my Game Boy."

"Your Game Boy?" Art said. "You play that by yourself, moron."

"Don't you think I know that, moron? That's why I brought it."

"Nice," Art said.

"We could always play my game," Lily said. "I mean, since we don't have anything else to do."

"What did you bring?" Joe and Art said together. They were giving her the same suspicious look.

"Monopoly," Lily said.

Joe's eyes narrowed. "What kind of Monopoly?"

"If you say Barbie, man, I am so out of here," Art said.

"Are ya'll talkin' about Barbie Monopoly?" Torie said. She stepped up next to Art, Angel situated on her hip the same way the basketball was placed on Joe's. "I used to love that when I was a kid! I haven't played that for so long!"

"I brought it with me," Lily said.

"You are *not* serious!"

"Yup."

"Well, bring it on, girl," Torie said. She looked at Angel. "This is going to be better than snow angels, baby. This has Barbie in it!"

"I like dat. Dat mine!" Angel said.

Joe gazed at Angel. "Hey, she talks," he said.

"She's not a moron, moron," Art said. Then he nudged Lily. "Go get your game. Me and Torie'll play you and Joe."

Yikes, Lily thought. *I think we oughta take Torie home with us. She's got him playing Barbie Monopoly now!*

They all went under the bleachers where they had been pulled out and set up the game there. After the licorice fiasco, Lily wasn't taking any chances on drawing a crowd.

Angel was fascinated by all the game pieces and the cards with Barbies on the backs of them. As she picked up each one of them, much to Lily's frustration, she said, "I like dat. Dat mine!"

"It's not actually yours," Lily said as she took yet another card out of Angel's hand. "It goes on this stack here, and everybody gets to play with it."

Angel smiled up at her and said, "Dat mine!"

"How about this?" Joe said, grabbing the toe of her sneaker. "Is this yours?"

"Ya," Angel said.

"What if I want it?" he said.

She shook her head. "Dat mine."

"What about this?" Joe pinched his nose. "Is this yours?"

"Ya. I like dat! Dat mine!"

She reached up and grabbed Joe's nose.

"Just don't grab hers," Lily said to Joe.

"Is it running again?" Torie said. "I'm already out of Kleenex."

"Hey, Angel," Joe said. "Just do like this." He dragged his sleeve under his nose.

"Gross me out and make me icky!" Lily said.

"That's what sleeves are for, right?" Joe said to Angel.

She nodded happily and crawled into Joe's lap.

Go figure, Lily thought as she laid out the dice on the game board. *Who'd have thought Joe would like a little kid?*

"All right," Torie said. "We roll to see who goes first."

"I go first, I'm the oldest," Art said.

"Art—we're playing by the rules," Lily said tightly.

"Would you rather arm wrestle for it?" Art said to Torie.

"I don't want to hurt you," Torie said.

"Okay—that sounds like a challenge," Art said, grinning. "Bring it on—come on, get your hand up here."

Lily sighed. "You gu-ys—"

But she stopped before the sentence even got started—because suddenly the gymnasium was plunged into darkness.

Chapter 8

It was the darkest dark Lily had ever seen. There was no light coming from anywhere, and for several seconds, she felt entirely alone. She reached out and found Art's knee.

"It's okay, Torie," Art said and put his hand over Lily's.

"It's me!" Lily said.

Just then Angel let out a whimper.

"Hey, Angel," Joe said. "Let's pretend we're hiding. That'll be cool."

"Who needs to hide?" Art said. "You could be an escaped felon in here."

"Thank you," Torie said. "That just put an image in my head I could do without."

Lily was amazed at how calm Torie sounded. Her own heart was racing, and beyond the bleachers, she could hear people shouting in worried voices. A couple of kids were crying.

"Listen to those little babies, Angel," Joe said. "They don't know how to be big like you."

Neither do I, Lily thought. *This is freaking me out!*

"Okay, the joke's over," Torie said. "Let's get those lights on."

"What do you want to bet the storm knocked out the electricity," Art said.

"Wonderful," Torie said. "Being stuck here wasn't enough. Now we have to be stuck—in the dark!"

Just then something groaned as if it were just waking up, and a dim light filtered between the benches above them. There was a weak cheer from the other part of the gym.

"All the way on would be nice," Art said. "Come on, you can do it."

"That's the generator," Torie said. "It only gives you enough light to see by."

"What about to cook by?" Joe said. "Man, I'm starving."

For the first time all day, Lily wasn't thinking about food. She scrambled to her feet and headed for Camp Robbins. Torie was right—there was barely enough light to see by—but she could make out Mom and Dad's shapes, and she was headed right for them.

"Taylor says the storm's knocked out the power lines," Dad was saying when she got there—with the rest of them on her heels. Torie was carrying the Barbie Monopoly game. Angel was riding on Joe's shoulders.

"This just keeps getting better and better, doesn't it?" Mom shook her head, bouncing her ponytail.

"I like dat—dat mine!" Angel said and made a lunge for Mom's hair. Joe was barely able to hang onto her.

"Who's this little person?" Mom said.

"This is Angel," Joe said. "Cool name, huh?"

"Oops—we have birthday candles coming out of our nose," Mom said. She pulled a Kleenex out of her sweats pocket and dabbed at Angel's nose. Angel didn't seem to notice; she was too fascinated by the ponytail.

"Get out your survival book, Hiker Adventure Barbie," Art said to Lily. "See if you can get us out of this one."

Lily could feel her shoulders sagging. She couldn't win.

"What survival book?" Torie said.

"Never mind," Lily said. "It wouldn't do us any good. I need a whole different book."

"Maybe you ought to try the one I brought," Dad said.

"We each had to bring one book," Art said to Torie.

"And only one," Joe put in.

Lily looked at her father. "You brought a survival book too?"

"I did," Dad said. "It tells you how to survive in any situation."

"Uh, we're not in Narnia anymore, Dad," Art said.

As he turned to tell Torie how into C. S. Lewis Dad was, Lily watched Dad reach into his bag and pull out a book she recognized right away. It was his Bible.

"Um, thanks," Lily said as he handed it to her, "but I don't think Jesus was ever stuck in a gym with no electricity and no food and no bed—"

"I think you'll find what you need in the sixth chapter of John," Dad said. "I'll even let you use the flashlight this time."

Angel stretched out her hands toward the Bible. "I like dat," she said. "Dat mine."

"You sound like my kids, Angel," Mom said. "Mine, mine, mine."

"Did we say that when we were little?" Joe said.

"I was talking about now, Joe," Mom said.

Lily decided this would not be a good time to say she didn't think the Bible was going to be much help. She sat down on the floor and thumbed through for John. To her surprise, Joe sat down across from her, still holding Angel.

"Wanna hear a story?" he said to her.

"Okay, who are you and what have you done with my brother?" Art said.

Torie sat down next to Joe so, of course, Art joined them.

"Read to us, Miss Lily," Torie said. "This'll be a switch. I'm usually the one reading the story—over and over and over." She looked at Angel, who was leaning against Joe, her thumb in her mouth. "Who says little children have short attention spans?"

"You guys really want to hear this?" Lily said.

"What else have we got to do?" Torie said.

Of course, Art said, "I'm in."

So Lily read the story about Jesus telling the disciples to feed the five thousand people who had come to hear him teach—none of whom had bothered to bring their lunches. None of them, that is, except a boy who had five small barley loaves and two small fish with him. He gave those to Jesus, who thanked God for them and then handed them out to everyone there—all five thousand of them—until they were all full.

"So where is Jesus when you need him, right?" Art said.

"He's here," Lily said. "I mean, you know, not *here* here, but here."

"Did you get that?" Joe said to Angel.

She took her thumb out of her mouth long enough to nod and then stuck it back in.

"Okay—yeah—Jesus is here," Art said. "But where's the kid with the order of fish and chips?"

Lily sat straight up.

"Uh-oh," Art said.

Torie looked at him. "What?"

"She has an idea. Not good."

"But it is good!" Lily said. "This one's really good! Why don't we do like the disciples and ask people to give us what they have? I bet if everybody in here gave us like one thing, we'd have a buffet."

"You can have *all* our squeeze cheese," Art said.

Angel rolled her eyes toward him and took her thumb out of her mouth.

"Yeah, I know," Art said. "You like dat—dat yours."

"So you're not saying Jesus is going to come in here and perform some miracle and my bag of Cheetos is going to turn into filet mignon for all, right?" Torie said. "You're just saying we're going to collect a bunch of food and have a potluck."

Torie's voice had its usual sarcastic edge, but her eyes were serious. For the first time, it occurred to Lily that Torie might not be a Christian—that this might have been the first time she'd ever heard the loaves and fishes story. It might sound a little far-out to her.

"A miracle *could* happen," Lily said.

"It's gonna *take* a miracle to get food out of some of these people," Art said. He looked at Torie. "You be the one to ask your mom, okay?"

"Aa-art!" Lily said.

But Torie was grinning at him. "You better watch it, boy. Like mother, like daughter, you know."

Why is she joking around with him? Lily thought. *I'd deck him if he said something like that about me.*

"Find anything helpful?" Dad said from where he'd suddenly appeared behind Joe.

Lily told him their idea and waited, biting on her lip, until he gave the okay.

"Mom and I'll set up some tables for you," Dad said.

"You'll probably only need one," Art said.

"Don't be such a pessimist," Torie said. "I like Lily's approach—she thinks positive."

That was all it took to get Lily up and running. She and Joe, with Angel in tow, teamed up and took one end of the gym, while Art and Torie worked on the other.

The first two families they went to weren't helpful. One man said they hadn't brought any food—although Lily was sure she'd smelled tortilla chips in their area—and right now she was so hungry she was sure she could have smelled applesauce through a refrigerator door. The second group said they would just as soon keep their food to themselves, thank you.

"There's some pretty stingy people here, Angel," Joe whispered to her as they walked away. "Everything's mine, mine, mine."

"Dat mine," Angel echoed faintly.

Lily felt herself start to struggle, but once again she straightened her shoulders. *I bet it took Jesus a couple tries to get that bread to multiply,* she thought. *I have to do like Torie said—I have to stay positive.*

In front of her, Joe stopped. "It's the old guy," he said in a low voice. "I bet he doesn't even have anything."

"Probably not," Lily said. He was so thin that she doubted whether he ate much even when he wasn't stuck in a high school gym.

Just as she was about to veer around him, the old man looked up from the lower bench of the bleachers, and his face broke into its crackly smile.

"There's my guardian angel," he said to Lily.

Angel grinned and waved at him.

"She thinks you're talking to her," Joe said. "Her name's Angel."

"And I bet she is one," the old man said. He turned to Lily. "You know, darlin', I was a little befuddled last night when you gave me your mat I didn't even introduce myself. I'm Wallace Chamberlain."

Lily introduced herself and Joe, who then introduced him to Angel again. The thought went through Lily's mind that pretty soon they were going to have to have Joe and Angel surgically removed from each other.

"Now," Mr. Chamberlain said. He folded his hands, which looked too gnarled to fit together anymore. "You were so kind to me last night. What can I do for you today?"

Lily looked at Joe. He lifted his eyebrows as if to say, *Who'd have thought?*

"We're asking people if they want to contribute any food to our buffet," Lily said. "It's gonna be for everybody. So if you give one thing you'll be able to sample a whole lot of different things—we hope."

Lily's voice trailed off, but Mr. Chamberlain slowly smiled again. "Now, you know," he said. "I never go far from home without taking along a picnic. 'Course, I've eaten most of it already. I wasn't planning to be gone this long—but what I have left is yours. Will some sardines, crackers, and hot mustard help?"

Except for the crackers, it sounded pretty gross to Lily. But then again, it was food.

"We would love to have it," she said.

"And it would be an honor to give it to you," Mr. Chamberlain said. "Give me a minute to dig it out—"

It took him a while—everything seemed to take him a while—but he finally handed over several cans of sardines, a box of crackers, and a half jar of hot mustard.

"That's been opened," he said, pointing to the jar. "I used it on my soft pretzels, but it's still fresh."

"Thank you so much!" Lily said.

Joe started off across the gym floor with Angel still on his shoulder to tell Torie and Art. Angel twisted around to look at the stash in Lily's hands and wailed, "I like dat! Dat mi-i-ine!"

If nobody else eats it, you can have it, Lily thought.

But obviously not everybody felt that way. After Torie arranged the whole thing on the lid to a cookie can she had and Art strode to the table with it, carrying it like a waiter would carry a tray, ears—and noses—began to perk up.

"Is that sardines?" somebody said.

"Don't tell me you have hot mustard," somebody else said. "I'd kill for some hot mustard. If I have to eat another Vienna sausage plain, I'm gonna—"

"If you're willing to share your sausages with everybody," Art said, "you're welcome to some hot mustard."

The woman stood up, three cans of Vienna sausages in hand. After that, it *was* like a miracle was taking place.

Several bags of chips appeared—one of them accompanied by a jar of salsa.

Five different packages of cookies made their way to the table.

Art and Torie collected a jar of olives, a whole Tupperware container full of homemade brownies with green and red sprinkles, and a discount-store-sized bag of candy canes.

Lily and Joe—and Angel—harvested a dozen oranges, a bag of pecans, four bottles of generic soda (but who cared?), and a fruit cake, which the guy who gave it to them said he was sure his mother wasn't going to like anyway.

One lady said she didn't have any food to contribute, but she did have a couple of candles they could use for the table. Some other people said if they were going to have candles, they were going to need a tablecloth, and gave up six rolls of Christmas wrapping paper for that purpose.

When it was all put together, Lily was amazed. It looked better than the buffet at the Londonshire. She even thought she might try the sardines.

"Hey!" somebody said.

The kids turned around to see a young man in workout clothes and a towel around his neck running toward them.

"I was in the weight room, and I heard you guys wanted food donations. This is all I got, man."

He pulled out a can of Dr. Pepper.

Art thanked him as he scooped it out of his hands and presented it to Torie.

"You are *not* serious," she said.

"Well, yeah," Art said. "I told you a miracle could happen."

No, I told her, Lily almost said. But she closed her mouth. Things were going so well—why push it?

Things *were* going well. The candles flickered as kids raced past, squealing and laughing for the first time all day. People who had been huddled in their little family camps were milling around, paper-towel-plates in hand, asking strangers questions like "Where are you from?" as they ate squeeze cheese and sardines.

The guy in the gym shorts who had provided the miracle Dr. Pepper for Torie pulled out a guitar and played a rock version of "Deck the Halls," which, Lily thought, would have gotten Art more interested if he weren't so busy checking out Torie. Actually, Lily was sure they'd gotten beyond that stage. They were sitting together on the end of the bleachers hanging onto every word the other one said. But she didn't know what this new stage was called.

Joe was still carting Angel around piggyback, but her head was lolling on his shoulder, and every few minutes her eyes would roll up into her head.

"Somebody's tired," Mom said.

"Nah—you're not tired, are ya, Angel?" Joe said. "You don't wanna go to bed."

Angel shook her head, just as her eyelids drifted closed.

"Victoria!" Cherise yelled in her gravel voice. "This child needs to be put down for the night!"

Lily thought the same thing Art had muttered to her earlier: Why didn't Cherise do it herself? Why was Torie the automatic babysitter?

But it didn't seem to bother Torie any. She bolted up from where she was sitting with Art and came to scoop Angel into her arms.

"Come on, baby," she said into her little pink ear. "You can practice your snow angels in your bed."

Cherise opened her mouth as Torie carried Angel off toward the Duncans' camp, but Mom put her hand on her arm.

"It looks like everyone's finished eating," Mom said. "You want to help me figure out a way to store all this leftover food? We might need it tomorrow morning if we're still here."

"We're gonna need a lot more than that," Cherise said. "No offense or anything—ya'll are obviously pretty religious, and that's fine—but we aren't gonna be able to keep pulling food out of nowhere. What I want to know is where is the Red Cross? They better have declared this an official disaster area by now."

"God's provided so far," Mom said—without a twitch in sight. "I think we can count on him to send in the Red Cross or—"

"Is God gonna get me to New York in time for Christmas?" Cherise said. She glanced at her watch. "I don't think so."

By then Torie had reappeared, and Art put his arm around her. "Do you sing?" he said.

"Yeah," she said. "Unless somebody pays me to shut up."

Art nodded his head toward the guitar player, who by now had gathered a crowd. "Let's go see if we can get anybody to pay up."

They moved off, but not before Torie looked at Cherise. So did Lily. Cherise was glaring at her daughter so hard that Lily was surprised Torie didn't end up with a hole burned in her forehead.

"Stay out of trouble," Cherise said.

What trouble is she gonna get into singing "Away in a Manger?" Lily thought. For about the sixteenth time that day, she thanked God that Cherise wasn't *her* mother.

Standing next to Lily, Joe sighed.

"It sure is boring around here without Angel," he said. "You wanna play some basketball?"

"Me?" Lily said. "No, I'd rather be shot."

For an instant—and no longer—a hurt look flickered through Joe's eyes, and Lily was sorry. Even after it was gone and Joe shrugged and slunk off, something flickered through Lily. *I wonder if I looked like that when he said he wouldn't play Barbie Monopoly with me if his life depended on it.*

"Hey, Joe," she said.

"What?" he said without looking back at her.

"I'm not any good at it—but I could try."

He did look at her then, and she could see him having an argument with himself. Finally he shrugged again, and said, "Okay. But you gotta let me show you how to shoot. You can't shoot like a girl, or you'll never make it."

"I *am* a girl," Lily said.

But her words were lost in a shriek that pierced the gym from one end to the other and brought the guitar to a halt in mid-chord.

"She's gone!" Torie was screaming. "Angel's gone!"

Chapter 9

There was a stunned silence, and then Cherise began to shriek. Between her and Torie, it sounded like something on the Discovery Channel. Finally, Mom got Cherise by the arm, and Dad put his arm around Torie's shoulders. They stopped screaming, but both of them were wild-eyed as Mom talked calmly.

"She isn't in her bed?" Mom said.

"No!" Torie said. "I went over to make sure she was still asleep, and she was gone! I looked all over—we have to find her!"

"Okay—we will," Mom said, and Dad squeezed Torie's shoulders.

"She's in here someplace—where's she gonna go?" Cherise said. And then in the next breath she added, "You should have sat there with that baby. No—I should have stayed with her myself— I knew you couldn't—"

"Let's spread out and search the gym," Mom said. "There are a lot of little nooks and crannies in here."

She let go of Cherise's arm and started sending people off in various directions. Art grabbed Torie's hand.

"Come on," he said. "We'll look together."

"Cherise," Dad said, "is the baby strong enough to push open the door that goes out into the hall?"

"Heaven only knows. Torie probably let her try it so she knows how they open. She hasn't got a lick of sense when it comes to that child."

"I showed her how they open," said a quiet little voice.

Lily looked at Joe. His face was pale, and his eyes were huge. He looked like he was on the verge of tears.

Cherise was already boring down on Joe with her eyes, so Lily said quickly, "Dad? Is there anything in the Bible for this situation?"

"This is *not* the time to be preaching a sermon!" Cherise shouted. "Where is that *baby*?"

Dad put one hand on Lily's shoulder and one on Joe's, but his eyes were on Cherise as he said, "There are a number of stories about lost children. God cares about every one of them. We'll find her."

Art hurried up just then, still holding Torie tightly by the hand. She was crying, and her lower lip was trembling hard. Although Lily had *told* her younger sibling to get lost a number of times, her heart went out to Torie. She wanted to cry herself, and as she opened her eyes wide to keep that from happening, she found Torie looking at her.

"Lily," she said in a voice thick with tears, " you need to pray for another one of those miracle things."

Lily felt her face going blotchy. It hadn't even occurred to her yet to pray. *We shoulda done that first,* she thought.

By now, Cherise had stalked off to question Mr. Selby, who had apparently just heard the news and was mobilizing a group of his volunteers to start searching the rest of the school. Lily took Torie's hand, the one Art wasn't holding, and said, "Come on—we'll pray."

"Art," Dad said, "let's help these guys."

Art managed to peel himself away from Torie, and Lily led her to the place on the bleachers where they'd first met, where Lily had given Angel her last piece of licorice. She wished now that being without candy was her biggest problem.

Lily took Torie by both hands as they sat down, and she bowed her head. She could feel Torie hesitating a little and then lowering her head too.

"What do I do?" Torie whispered.

"I'll just talk to God like I always do," Lily said, "and if you feel like saying something you can. Or you can just listen. He likes both."

Lily began to pray, pouring out all the fear and confusion and begging God for help in finding his little Angel. She could feel Torie's hands relaxing in hers.

Lily had just gotten to the Amen when she felt footsteps jarring the floor nearby. She looked up in time to see Cherise grab Torie by the arm and jerk her to her feet.

"What are you *doing?*" she screamed.

"We were—"

"You *better* be getting up off your tail and finding that kid—and then we *are* taking her to Kathy and Warren's and there isn't gon' be no more argument over it—because I've had it with you. Now *get!*"

With that, Cherise drew back a hand and smacked sixteen-year-old Torie so hard on the backside, Lily felt the sting. Lily stared down at her lap until Torie hurried away. If it had been her, Lily wouldn't have wanted anybody looking at her.

But Lily could feel Cherise's glare on *her,* and she had to get out from under it. She stood up to go. Cherise put her hand out so that Lily ran into it, chest first.

"Why don't you just stay out of the way, little girl?" Cherise said. "You don't know nothin' about this. Just stay out of the way."

Cherise stomped off with a swish of her satin jacket, and Lily sank back down on the bench. There wasn't a place on her that wasn't stinging.

Cherise had just talked to her the way she talked to Torie and Angel—*get out of the way—you have no responsibility—you're useless—you're stupid.*

No wonder the kid went off and hid someplace, Lily thought angrily. *I'd want to get away from a mother like that too.*

Except that Angel was too little to be off by herself somewhere. She was probably—Lily stopped in mid-thought. *That* was the problem. They were all thinking like bigger kids or adults would think—not the way a baby like Angel would.

In the first place, she was a lot lower to the ground, so her hiding places would be down there too. Lily scrambled from the bench and lay down on the floor and looked around. Things were definitely different from the Angel point of view. What had she been thinking while she was lying on her little pallet down here?

She was probably doing snow angels, Lily thought. *That's what Torie told her to do.*

Lily was about to do one herself when it came to her. Angel had wanted to do snow angels so badly. Lily sat up straight. The Duncans' camping site wasn't far from the door that led outside. If Joe had told her about the hallway doors, he'd probably filled her in on that one too, complete with instructions on how to open it.

Lily looked frantically around the gym, but everyone seemed to have gone off on the school-wide search. Stopping only to grab her jacket, she went for the door, opened it merely by pushing down on the bar, and stepped outside.

The snow was still coming down so hard that at first Lily couldn't see anything but swirling white. It was getting dark, too, and Lily had to step forward to even see the trees. She let the door shut behind her and picked her way out into the storm.

"An-gel!" she cried.

The sound of her voice seemed to fall dead in the wind, but she tried again, over and over. "Angel! Angel—it's Lily! Are you out here?"

If she is, she must be terrified by now, Lily thought, because she herself felt small and helpless in the face of the blistering cold wind and the flying snow that stung her face like Cherise's words. Maybe this hadn't been a good idea—maybe she should go back inside and get somebody to come out with her.

Lily made her way back to the door and pulled on the handle. The door didn't budge. She pulled twice more before she remembered what Mr. Selby had told them last night. "Don't go out unless you've made arrangements for somebody to let you back in," he'd said. "The doors lock from the inside automatically."

Lily pounded on the door until her hands hurt, but no one seemed to hear her. Her hands were so cold without gloves she finally had to stuff them back into her pockets. She prayed that the pain would go away.

In fact, she prayed for a lot of things—for somebody to let her in—for Angel to already have been found—for this snow to stop so they could all go home.

Except for Torie and Angel. Why would they want to go home? And would Angel be going home at all? It had sounded like Cherise intended to dump her off with somebody named Kathy and Warren.

It all sounded so lonely and harsh that Lily couldn't stand it any longer. She turned toward the building and, cold or not, banged on the door with both fists.

"Let me in!" she shouted. "Somebody let me in!"

She kept on until her hands hurt again. She sagged with her back against the door as she stuffed them into her pockets and looked miserably through the snow.

I know how you feel, Angel, she thought. *I feel lost too.*

Lily was about to close her eyes and pray again when something red caught her eye on the top of the blanket of white. What could it be that wasn't already buried in snow?

Leaning into the wind, Lily stumbled toward it and reached down for it. It was Angel's red blanket.

Lily picked it up and whirled around, already shouting Angel's name again. There was no answer, but she couldn't be far. The snow had barely started to cover it up.

Lily suddenly dropped to her knees in the snow and searched. The snow had begun to bury the tiny footprints, but there were enough of them for Lily to tell that she'd wandered away from the direction of the building when she'd dropped her blanket.

"I sure hope Torie left her shoes on her," Lily said out loud. It was so lonely out here—so empty—it helped to talk. She kept on chattering as she followed the little dents in the snow.

"I'm on your trail now, girlfriend. I don't blame you for wanting to get away, but you gotta go back. You're too little to be out here by yourself." Lily grunted. "*I'm* too little to be out here by myself!"

Forcing herself to keep her head up as the snow froze her face, Lily stopped and put her hand up to shield her eyes so she could search. She turned her head one way and then the other—and she saw it.

It was just movement at first, and then Lily could tell it was little Angel, pulling herself up from where she'd been lying in the snow, and toddling still further from the school—and further from Lily.

Lily pulled her hands out of her pockets and was about to take off after her when she heard a noise behind and above her. It took a moment to get turned around because the snow was past her knees and it was hard to maneuver. Even as she turned, the noise kept up. It was screaming and banging, and it seemed to be coming from a window, high up in the gym.

It was getting even darker now, and Lily had to squint to see. The ghostly generator lights outlined three forms in the window—two tall and slender, another short. The way they were frantically banging and screaming and gesturing to her, she was sure it was Art and Torie and Joe.

Lily surrounded her mouth with her hands and yelled, "I found her! Don't worry! I found her!"

She got herself turned around again to go after Angel, who she could still see tottering down a little hill. She disappeared for a moment, and Lily did some high stepping in an attempt to run to her—but she fell face forward in the snow. Even as she scrambled up and kept on, she knew what Angel was doing. She was stopping every few feet now to make angels in the snow.

That oughta slow her down, Lily thought as she plowed forward.

Behind and above her, the screaming and the banging continued. Lily turned only the upper part of her body toward them and pointed with big exaggerated arms to where Angel was once again getting to her feet. But her pointing seemed to make Art and Torie and Joe more frantic than ever. Torie was shaking her head, and Art was crossing both arms in front of him over and over. Joe was hurling himself against the glass like he wanted to go through it.

"For Pete's sake," Lily said. "What is the deal?"

She turned again to go, because Angel appeared to be picking up her pace as she half walked, half slid down the little hill. But it was clear that if Lily didn't stop and look at the three in the window, Joe *was* going to crash himself through it.

Sighing, Lily held out both arms and shrugged her shoulders. "What are you saying?" she shouted at them.

Torie and Joe were jumping up and down. Art put his hands on both their heads and they stopped. Art pointed in Angel's direction, brought first one arm over his head and then forward, and then did the same with the other one. He looked like he was trying to swim.

"She's not swimming!" Lily shouted at them. "Where's she gonna swim—she's—"

And then she stopped cold—frozen by the words she'd heard only hours before. *There's a lake on campus, which has frozen over—it isn't safe to walk on—it's covered in snow, so it's hard to even see it until you're on top of it.*

Lily's hand went to her mouth. Up in the window, Art nodded until she thought his head would roll off. Then, in a flash of fear, Lily came unfrozen and hurtled forward in the snow toward little Angel and the frozen lake—the thinly frozen lake.

Chapter

10

Lily's thoughts were screaming as she took the distance between herself and Angel in bounds and slides and jumps that landed her headfirst in the snow.

Am I gonna get there before she goes through the ice and drowns? Why don't Art and them come down here and help me? Why didn't they come down here and tell me? Why don't they send Dad or somebody?

There was only one answer to that, and Lily knew it as she made the last leap toward Angel. They didn't come down because they couldn't. They'd obviously gotten themselves locked in up there. Every door must lock from the inside.

Lily didn't have time to think about that. Just as she reached out with both hands to grab Angel, trying not to screech as she said, "Hey, Angel! Come with me!"—Angel took a few more steps and fell. She didn't plunk down in the snow, however. The snow itself was only a few inches deep where she fell—and she slid crazily on her little backside. As if she were on ice.

Lily lurched to a stop and stared down in horror. She could see in the last snow angel the little girl had made about a foot away from where Lily was standing that she was right on the edge of the frozen lake. And Angel was out *on* it—by several yards—and sliding farther away by the second.

"Angel!" Lily screamed. "Come back this way! You're gonna fall through and drown! Angel!"

She could hear her own voice flying out of control. Angel must have sensed it, too, because she put her hands down on the snowy ice and looked at Lily. Even through the blowing snow and the growing darkness, Lily could see the merriment slip out of her big dark eyes. Lily forced herself to take a breath and speak more softly.

"That's fun, huh, Angel?" she said. Her voice was shaking, but it was the best she could do. "But you can't make snow angels out there. You can only make them up here—where it's deep."

She waited. Angel blinked at her, looked down at the few inches of snow she was sitting in, and flopped down on her back.

"No!" Lily cried. So much for softness. She didn't dare look back up at the window. Joe was probably getting a running start at the glass right about now.

"No," Lily said, pulling her voice back as much as she could. She could hear the tears in it. "Angel—you're gonna get hurt—uh—" *What was it Torie called her? Baby.* "You're gonna get hurt, baby. Come on—come up here, and I'll play with you."

That got Angel to sit up, but she didn't come any closer. She just blinked at Lily.

If I were Joe she'd already be over here, Lily thought. But she kept coaxing—and Angel kept blinking.

"Okay, this isn't working," Lily said. She took another deep breath—and then another—until she realized she was gasping for air.

Calm down! she told herself firmly. *God—you gotta help me calm down—please. I can't let this little kid die—please—help me!*

She took another deep breath—but there wasn't another one. Lily stayed still for a moment and tried to think.

That survival book had sure been no help. The only thing she could remember from the Bible right now was Jesus walking on water—and she didn't dare do that. She went back to the survival book in her head. All she could remember was BE RESOURCEFUL.

Lily looked around wildly. Okay. What if she had something to lure Angel with? Too bad she'd already given her that last piece of licorice. There was nothing but whiteness out here—

Except for one spot of red.

"Angel!" Lily said. She tried to make her voice sing-songy. That made Angel giggle. So far—so good. "Angel!" Lily sang out again. "Stay right there. I'm gonna get you a surprise!"

That at least got her attention. The dark eyes were blinking in anticipation as Lily tore back through the snow toward the red blanket. It wasn't so hard this time—she'd left a trail for herself and besides, she was far too frantic to let a little knee-high snow slow her down.

She didn't even stop when she reached the blanket but snatched it up and hauled herself back toward the lake. To her relief, Angel hadn't moved. She hadn't come any closer to the edge of the lake, but she hadn't wandered farther off, either.

"Look what I got!" she said, dangling the red blanket like a carrot in front of her. "You want your blankie?"

"I like dat!" Angel chirped. "Dat mine!"

"Then come get it!" Lily said. She squatted down and held the blanket out in front of her. "Come over here, and I'll give it to you."

"Dat mine!" Angel said, and she struggled to her feet and began to toddle toward Lily. She hadn't taken two steps before her feet flew out from under her, and she landed on her tummy. The ice was clear in that spot, and her little bare hands slapped on it hard.

There was a moment in which Lily and Angel were both paralyzed. Then Angel drew up her face and began to squall.

"It's okay, Angel!" Lily said, though from the way the baby was crying, it was obviously far from okay. Lily could almost feel Angel's hands stinging as she lay there with her palms flat on the ice. For the first time, Lily realized that Angel wasn't wearing a coat—or a hat—and certainly not mittens. She'd been having so much fun that she probably hadn't realized it herself until now. Now it was all pain, and she was crying harder by the second.

"It's okay, Angel!" was all Lily could think of to say as she closed her eyes and tried once more to be resourceful. She couldn't leave Angel out there crying, even to go bang on the door again. She glanced back up at the window, but it was so dark, she couldn't see it anymore. Angel took a huge, choking breath and started in anew.

Lily took a breath of her own and reached out from her squatting position and tested the ice with her hand. It seemed solid enough. Maybe if she didn't put all of her weight on it—maybe if she just got her upper body out there, Angel would feel like she was closer and come to her. Or maybe Lily could even reach her.

Lily zipped up her jacket and eased herself slowly down onto the ice, chest first. The snow plowed out from her sides, and she could feel the hardness of the lake under her.

"Just don't let it break, God," she whispered. "Just please don't let it break."

Keeping her hips and legs firmly on solid ground, Lily inched the upper part of her body out onto the ice the way she'd seen Joe do when he used to play soldier in the back yard. Her left hand was already searing with pain, but the right one still clung to the blanket. When Lily got out as far as she dared and could still feel her legs and feet buried in snow, she stretched her left hand out and tried to reach Angel. She was still about a foot short.

"Crawl to me, baby," Lily said above the howling of the wind and the even louder howling of the baby. "Your blankie will make you feel better."

In fact, Angel was now staring at the blanket through her tears. "Dat mine!" she wailed.

"I know!" Lily said. "And I'm not just keeping it from you to be mean, I promise. I'm not like your mom—"

"Mom-meee!" Angel cried.

Lily could have bitten her tongue off. "I'll take you to see Mommy, I promise," she said.

"Mommy mine!" Angel screamed. Her voice was getting higher and more panicky. "DAT mine!"

She lunged for the blanket, but her little hand missed it. The move, however, had brought her about six inches closer. She was just within reach.

Lily breathed a silent prayer and slowly, carefully inched herself out onto the ice. Her legs and feet were no longer in the snow, but she could reach Angel. She pulled her forward by both arms.

Angel squalled and, to Lily's horror, began to kick.

"No!" Lily said. "Here's your blanket—see—here it is. Let's go see Mommy!"

In spite of the tantrum Angel was suddenly throwing, Lily managed to pull Angel's face into the blanket and get the rest of her turned around so that Lily was lying on her side on the ice, holding Angel against her. The minute the baby got a whiff of the red blanket, she relaxed, and her crying settled into a long, low whimper.

"Okay," Lily said to her. "Stay really still like that, and I'm gonna turn us around. We're just gonna spin around really slow and get headed back in the right direction—"

Holding onto Angel with both arms so she couldn't wriggle away, Lily used her feet to move herself in a circle, like the spinner on a board game. It seemed to take forever, especially with her cheek smashed against the ice, but finally Lily could see the school building again. It suddenly looked like the Marriott Hotel to Lily. No—it looked like home, and she wanted to get there.

Lily let go of Angel with one arm so she could pull herself forward with the other. They just had a few more feet to go—and then a few inches. The deep snow was so close Lily could almost feel herself sinking into it. The relief was already pumping in her face.

"We're there, Angel!" she cried, and she let her foot do the final push.

The ice gave way under it, and frigid water pulled at Lily's pant leg.

"No!" Lily cried.

But the ice paid no attention, and beneath her other leg, it broke through as well. Lily could feel her lower body sinking, and she couldn't stop it.

"Go, Angel!" she shouted, and she thrust Angel forward like a basketball. The baby landed face first in the snow, screaming and kicking her feet.

Lily kicked hers, too, trying to lift herself out of the water. She groped and grabbed with her hands, but they only slid back to her on the ice, just inches from the edge of the lake.

"Help!" she screamed. "Somebody help—somebody!"

All she could do was scream and kick. On the shore, Angel screamed with her.

And then someone else was screaming too.

"Lily! Hold on, Lily—we're coming!"

It was Art—or at least it sounded like Art. It was hard to tell in the chaos of shouting that seemed to be going on behind him. But Lily zoned in on his voice, and she screamed even louder.

"Art—help me! I'm falling through the ice!"

And then he was there, his face barely inches from hers as he threw himself down and thrust out his arm.

"Grab on!" he said.

Lily could barely get her hand to obey, but she reached out numbly. Her arm felt like a piece of frozen wood as Art took it with both hands and pulled. Her chest came up off the ice, but her legs were heavy in the water.

"I can't!" she cried.

"Yes, you can!" another voice called out. And then there were more arms grabbing her—around her shoulders and under her arms and at the back of her jacket.

Someone yelled "Now!"—and Lily was out of the water.

From then on, everything moved slowly, like the air rising from a freezer.

Someone carried her into the gym, and someone else ripped off her clothes. She hurt too much to wonder if everybody in the school was watching. She was just so glad for the blankets and blankets and more blankets several people rolled her in. Lily couldn't feel her legs, but she welcomed the hat someone pulled down over her ears.

In the distance, she could hear Angel squalling, only she sounded mad now, rather than terrified.

"Is Angel okay?" Lily said—or at least, she tried to say it. Her lips were almost too stiff to move.

"She's fine," Dad said.

"She's a little ticked off right now," Joe said. "'Cause they got her arms all stuffed down in a sleeping bag and she can't get 'em out."

Lily hugged her own arms against her and felt suddenly sleepy.

"I survived," she said, though she hadn't planned to say that.

"Yes, thank the Lord," Mom said.

"But I don't think I wanna be Outdoor Woman anymore. I'm glad you didn't buy me all that stuff after all."

From somewhere far away, somebody laughed at that, but Lily didn't know whom. She was already falling asleep.

She didn't sleep for long, because Mom woke her up and made her sit up and drink a cup of coffee with milk and sugar.

"I hate coffee," Lily said.

"It's the only thing hot we have right now, and I want to be sure we get your body temperature back up," Mom said.

"Go ahead, Lil," Art said. "It'll put hair on your chest."

He was sitting on the floor near her, with Joe beside him. They were both looking at her as if she were a TV program.

"What?" she said. "Do I have a booger coming out of my nose? Somebody could have told me—"

"No—we're just waiting to see if any of your fingers fall off," Art said, grinning.

"Yeah," Joe said. "That would be so cool."

"Get out of here, both of you," Mom said. "Go tell Torie that Lily's awake. She wanted to talk to her."

"I bet Torie's in *so* much trouble with Cherise," Lily said when they were gone. "I hope she didn't hit her again."

"Hit her?" Mom said.

"Again?" Dad said.

They had an eye conversation while Lily sipped at the coffee and made a face.

"Hey," said a voice above them.

It was Torie. She dropped to her knees beside Lily and flung both arms around her. Mom barely rescued the coffee in time.

"Thank you," Torie said into Lily's hair. Lily could tell she was still crying. "Thank you so, *so* much. You saved my little girl."

Lily cocked her head as Torie pulled away and sat back on her heels. "It really is like she's yours, huh?" Lily said. "Your mom makes you take care of her all the time."

Torie looked down at her hands and then at Mom and Dad. Mom nodded at her.

"What?" Lily said.

"It's okay, Torie," Dad said. "You can tell Lily and Joe."

"Tell us what?" Lily said.

Torie looked Lily straight in the eyes, as if she were about to say something difficult and she only wanted to say it once. "Angel *is* mine," she said. "I had her when I was fourteen."

Lily felt her eyes widening. "Did you get married when you were, like, thirteen or something?"

"I wasn't married," Torie said. "I was just stupid."

"Oh," Lily said.

"I can't imagine what my life would be like without her now, so I can't thank you enough for saving her. I really can't."

Then Torie suddenly got up and hurried off, back to Angel.

"Evidently her *mother* can imagine Torie's life without Angel," Art said when she was gone.

Lily looked quickly at Art. His voice sounded bitter, and his face matched it. He was clenching and unclenching his fists. Evidently, he'd known about Torie and Angel longer than Lily had.

"What's that mean?" Joe said.

"Torie's mother doesn't think she can take care of Angel," Mom said, "so they're taking her to New York to some relatives who don't have any children of their own."

"Angel doesn't want to live with Kathy and Warren!" Lily said. "She wants to be with Torie!"

"Why can't we adopt her?" Joe said. "You guys want to adopt some kid—why can't we take Angel?"

"It doesn't exactly work that way, son," Dad said. "If Angel were being abused or neglected that would be one thing, but Torie's mother has the right to make decisions for her welfare—and Angel's."

"That's not fair," Joe said. "Angel already knows us. I betcha she's never even seen those Warren people. She'd be *so* much better off with us. We got a good family."

"Maybe Katie and Will do too," Dad said. "We have to trust God on this."

"Who's Katie and Will?" Art said.

"Kathy and Warren," Mom said. "And you know what, guys—we do have a good family—and right now I think we all ought to try to get some sleep."

"Mom?" Lily said as her mom started to stand up.

"What do you need, Lil?" Mom said.

"I need all you guys to sleep here close to me," she said.

Dad chuckled. "Like a litter of puppies."

"Only if Art doesn't breathe bad breath on me," Joe said. And to Lily's surprise, that was the only protest he made as he pulled his pallet closer.

Within a few minutes, the Robbins were huddled together, with pallets touching. Mom had a hand on Lily on one side and Dad had one on her on the other. She felt them both go limp as they fell asleep. Lily herself was awake for a long time, thanking God that this was her family. It was all she needed for Christmas.

Chapter 11

It stopped snowing during the night, and when Lily woke up just before noon the next day, people were packing up, and some had already been taken back to their cars so they could try to dig out. The first family Lily looked for were the Duncans.

"Where's Torie and Angel?" she said.

Joe and Art's sullen faces answered the question.

"I didn't even get to say good bye," Lily said.

"Join the club," Art said. "I went in to take a shower, and when I came out, they were out of here."

"I only got to hold Angel for like two seconds and then that Cherise woman was all grumpin' at me," Joe said. He scowled darkly. "I still think *we* oughta adopt Angel."

I think I'll adopt you, Lily thought as she stared at Joe. *And then I'll hold onto you and hope that other Joe doesn't reappear.*

"I wish Mom and Dad would get back," Joe said. "I'm starving."

"Where'd they go?" Lily said.

"Mr. Selby took them to get McDonald's breakfast for us since we hafta hang around 'til they can get a tow truck to pull out the van," Art said.

Lily could feel her mouth watering. "You think pancakes?" she said.

"Mom said she was getting three or four of everything." Joe grinned slyly. "They were in a really good mood this morning."

Art grunted.

"You're not," Lily said to him. She got up on her elbows on her pallet and squirmed under the mountain of blankets. It suddenly occurred to her that the electricity was back on, and the heater was blasting in the gym. "Is it because Torie's gone?"

Art shrugged. "Kinda."

"I liked her too," Lily said. "Probably not the way you did—I guess—but didn't it seem like we knew her forever, even though it was like only one day?"

Art nodded absently, as if he hadn't really heard what she'd said. "I'm thinking about not dating so much from now on," he said. "I'm thinking about telling Marsha we shouldn't be so serious. Dude— we're only seventeen."

"Is that because of Torie?" Lily said.

"Because of what happened to Torie," Art said.

"What did happen to her anyway?" Joe said. "I didn't get that. Angel's not her sister, she's her kid?"

"Yeah—that can happen if you get into serious relationships when you're way too young," Art said. "I'm looking at Torie and I'm thinking no wonder God says don't be acting like you're married when you're not. Her life's all weird now because she's got Angel—and Angel's life's all weird. It's bad news."

"I still don't get it," Joe said.

"Dad'll explain it to you," Art said.

Wow, Lily thought as she watched the two of them. *All three of us just had an actual conversation. Nobody even insulted anybody else or said anything sarcastic.*

She would have savored it more, but Mom and Dad arrived just then, laden with about six McDonald's bags each. Lily spread out a blanket, and they had a picnic. Food had never tasted so good. Nobody even complained when they ran short of syrup.

"They've promised to have the car out by late this afternoon," Dad said as they were stuffing the empty containers back into the bags—and they were *all* empty. "Taylor has invited us to stay at his house tonight, and then we can head home tomorrow."

Mom's mouth twitched. "There will still be two days left for us to shop."

"Home?" Art said. "I thought we were going to a cabin in North Carolina."

"Well, we were, but—"

"Why can't we still go there?" Joe said.

"I already told you that I don't want all that camping stuff now," Lily said. "And besides, I already figured out what I'm gonna do for everybody for Christmas down there."

"All right, you bunch of imposters," Mom said. "Where are our real kids?"

"You seriously want to go to the cabin?" Dad said. "After all this?"

"Because of all this," Art said.

Dad leaned forward as if he were intrigued. "How so?" he said.

"Well—" Joe paused and looked at Lily. "You tell him, Lily."

"Because," Lily said. She twirled a red curl around her finger. "We went through all this, right? If we went back home, we might forget what you wanted us to learn, like, right away."

Mom and Dad looked at Art and Joe. They nodded.

"Go on," Dad said. If he'd been intrigued before, he was fascinated now.

"And we all just started to really get along," Lily said. "Me and Art and Joe quit fighting and stopped complaining about you guys. And we made, like, these sacrifices for other people, and that's the Christmas you wanted, right?"

Mom nodded, ponytail bouncing. Lily wasn't sure, but she thought Mom's eyes looked a little wet.

Art took up the thread from there. "If we go home right away, there's gonna be the TV and the phone—"

"And the refrigerator," Joe added.

"And we might slide right back into our old habits. This way, we have to keep doing this stuff." Art shrugged. "If you do something long enough, it starts to become a new habit. I figure we gotta give ourselves a chance."

"Besides," Joe said, "if it snowed this much down in North Carolina, we could build some major snowmen."

"And make snow angels," Lily said.

"Shut up!" Joe said. "That makes me think about Angel."

Mom grabbed Joe and pulled him into a hug. "I think you might be human after all, Joe," she said.

The tow truck people kept their promise, and the van was out of the ditch before dark. The best news was that there was no damage to it. The people at the garage said they would have the heater fixed by the next morning, and they did. After a breakfast of waffles and very salty ham in Mr. and Mrs. Selby's toasty kitchen, the Robbins took off for North Carolina in a warm van.

They stopped at a grocery store in the little town before they reached the cabin and bought enough food for, as Dad put it, Washington's army at Valley Forge. Then they spent the next three days eating it in front of the fireplace in the main room of the cabin.

"Cabin?" Mom said when they first walked in the door. "This is bigger than our house."

There was a loft room for each of the kids, but they didn't spend much time there. When they weren't eating, they were playing the board games they found in one of the cabinets, reading out loud from the collection of books that lined the walls, playing in the snow—no snow angels allowed—and decorating the place for Christmas Eve.

Just as Dad had said, they couldn't chop down a tree, but there were enough pine branches lying around to make garlands for the whole main room. It smelled better than any tree they'd ever bought. Lily put holly, laden with berries, in bowls around the place, and Dad hung up one of each of their socks above the fireplace. Joe and Art built an enormous snowman complete with carrot nose and a ball cap, compliments of Joe. The snowman was, of course, a Phillies fan.

They all took "alone time," as Lily called it, on Christmas Eve to prepare their presents for each other. Mom, Lily thought, must have been really into it, because she didn't cook anything that day. Maybe they were going to have their traditional dinner on Christmas Day instead of that night.

By the time it got dark, Dad had a roaring fire in the fireplace, and they all gathered so Dad could read the Christmas story from the

Bible. Even Joe listened to the whole thing without making any smart remarks. In fact, when Dad closed the Bible, Joe was unusually quiet.

"What's up?" Mom said, tousling his hair.

"What happened to Mary," Joe said, "when that angel came and told her she was gonna have a baby. She wasn't even married—that's kind of what happened to Torie."

"Not exactly," Dad said slowly.

"I know not exactly," Joe said, rolling his eyes. "But I mean, Mary was like all freaked out at first, and Torie musta been too. Too bad she didn't have, like, a Joseph."

"You're scaring me, Joe," Mom said. "You're being way too sweet."

Joe grinned at her. "It's my Christmas present to you, Mom."

"Wonderful," Mom said, and she kissed him noisily on the cheek.

While he was wiping it off, Art said, "Speaking of presents, let's do the gift thing now. I'll go first."

He reached into his pocket and pulled out several pieces of paper, which he examined one by one and passed out to everyone.

"What is it?" Joe said.

"It's the song I'd dedicate to each one of you," Art said. "I woulda written one for everybody, but I don't have my guitar with me or anything."

"You write music, son?" Dad said.

"I just started," Art said. "I wrote this version of the Lord's Prayer—well, I'll play it for you when we get home."

Mom and Dad looked mistily at each other. Lily unfolded her paper. "I Love You Just the Way You Are," it said. "By Billy Joel."

"I think I got the wrong one," Lily said.

Art glanced at it and shook his head. "No," he said. "That one's yours."

"Oh," Lily said. "Wow." It was better than a six-person tent *or* a rain poncho—or both of those put together.

Joe handed his out next. He'd made leather friendship bracelets for all of them.

"I hate to look a gift horse in the mouth," Mom said, "but where did you get the leather?"

"Off my shoes and stuff," Joe said. "I'm gonna need to buy all new shoelaces when I get home."

"You were resourceful," Lily said.

"Oh," Joe said. "Thanks—I guess."

Dad had written each of them a poem. Joe's was funny. Art's was witty and intellectual sounding. Mom's was romantic. But Lily was certain hers was the best.

> *You said, "We should pray."*
> *I hugged the words to my chest*
> *Like a down pillow.*
> *You bowed your head down,*
> *Your hands wrapped up in her hands,*
> *And spoke like velvet.*
> *Your cheekbones shimmered,*
> *Skin the color of God*
> *As you prayed with her.*
> *"She knows him," I said.*
> *"Like a child knows a mother's voice*
> *She truly knows him."*

"My gifts are not nearly so creative," Mom said. "Or sentimental—"

"Quit apologizing, Mom," Art said. "Whatcha got?"

Mom handed them each a coupon she'd cut from paper and colored with some Crayons she'd found.

Dad's was good for private lessons in basketball.

Art's was good for a tank of gas when they got back home.

Joe could redeem his for a trip to the movies, where she promised to eat a package of Sour Patch Kids with him.

Once again, Lily privately thought the one she got was the absolute best. *Good for one Mom and Lily Only Saturday—since we survived three days alone in a cabin with these men.*

Lily started immediately concocting a whole day with Mom in her head.

Finally it was Lily's turn, and nobody seemed tired of the process yet. In fact, all eyes were on her, shining, as she pulled four medals out of her bag. They were fashioned from aluminum foil, and each was lettered with a Bible reference in nail polish. There was a mad scramble for the Bible as they looked them up.

"Mine's Psalm 33:1–3!" Art called out.

"Look up mine," Mom said. "Ruth 1:16–18."

Dad gave Lily an approving nod. "Proverbs 4:1–2. I already know what that is. Thank you, Lilliputian."

"Matthew 19:13–15," Joe said.

"That's the one about Jesus telling the disciples to let the children come to him—that they were important," Mom said.

Joe cocked his head to the side, and then he grinned. "I like dat," he said. "Dat mine."

His grin looked a little sad, and Lily felt bad for him. He must really miss Angel. She was trying to decide whether to reach over and hug him when there was a knock on the door. Art gave Lily a baffled look.

"Who even knows we're here?" he said.

Mom nudged Joe. "Check it out," she said.

Joe needed no further prodding to get to the door. When he flung it open, an aroma like no other flooded the room.

"Pizza!" Art, Joe, and Lily shouted together.

"Merry Christmas to you folks too," the delivery person said. "Sounds like ya'll are having a great Christmas."

"Oh, we are!" Lily said.

And then she whispered, "Thank you, God. It's the best one we've ever had."

the LILY series

If you liked *Rough & Rugged Lily*, you'll love its non-fiction companion *The Year 'Round Holiday Book*

THE YEAR 'ROUND HOLIDAY BOOK

it's a God thing!

Written by Nancy Rue
Illustrated by Lyn Boyer

Zonderkidz

Making Holidays Holy Days (Without Driving Everybody Nuts!)

Do this in remembrance of me.
1 Corinthians 11:24

Okay—time to be honest. How often do you look at the calendar to see how many school days there are until your next holiday? And how often does it matter to you what the holiday is, just as long as you get the day off?

Sure, you might like the Memorial Day picnic or the Veterans' Day parade, and maybe your mom bakes a cherry pie for Presidents' Day. But chances are, unless it's Christmas or Thanksgiving, you don't much care about the reason you get to sleep in!

However, there are some holidays that you might want to consider more carefully. Let's begin by looking at the word itself. *Holiday* is kind of a contraction—like *don't* for *do not*—for "holy day." Even though we now refer to practically any day we don't have to go to school as a holiday, originally holy days were just that—days for observing something holy, something that was of God.

Nowadays, some of those holy days, which started out being sacred (holy), have become secular (worldly). Christmas is a good example. This holy day, created to celebrate the birth of Christ, has now become pretty secular. Many people get so busy with cookies, elves, and reindeer that they barely give Jesus and the manger a passing thought. The same is true for Easter, with its bunnies and chicks and baskets of candy, and Halloween, which has become a celebration of all things creepy and scary and disgusting.

Not only that, some of the original holy days and seasons are no longer observed by many Christians. Ever heard of Epiphany or the Feast of Pentecost? Do you know what Advent is? (Hint: It isn't just a time for Christmas shopping.) And how about Lent? Are you thinking it might be that time of year when people give up stuff—like candy and gum, kind of like a diet before they hit the Easter basket? They aren't out-of-date holy days, noted only by those denominations that observe the church year. These special days are important for all Christians because they give us opportunities to remember and celebrate all the things God is in our lives.

Think what it would be like if you never had a day off from school—time to sit back and regroup and get revived for, well, more school. Holy days give us a chance to get juiced up about God so you can get out there and let God live in you and through you.

In this book, we'll take a look at five different holy days and seasons, starting with Advent, which is the spiritual preparation for Christmas. We'll explore Epiphany and then Lent, which is the spiritual preparation for Easter, before taking a look at the Feast of Pentecost. We'll even examine some holidays that aren't part of the church year but are important to us as Americans. We'll look at how all those holidays and seasons got started and how you can celebrate them in a sacred way that will bring you even closer to God—without driving your family whacko at the same time.

Notice that we aren't going to talk a lot about Christmas and Easter, because most families and churches have those pretty well covered. If you observe Advent and Lent, your Christmas and Easter are going to be God-times naturally.

Let's take a look at how these God-given opportunities for celebration work.

How Is This a God Thing?

When Jesus got together with his disciples in the upper room on the night before he died, he gave them some important instructions and showed them how to carry them out. Lifting up the bread, he gave thanks for it, broke it, and gave it to them. "This is my body given for you; do this in remembrance of me," he told them (Luke 22:19).

Then, picking up the cup of wine, he gave thanks for it and told his disciples to drink from that same cup. Then he told them, "This cup is the new covenant in my blood, which is poured out for you" (Luke 22:20).

Jesus was using the bread and wine as symbols of his body and blood, so that when he was gone, his friends would always remember that he lived on within them, strengthening them and helping them grow the way food helps our bodies to grow. He established a ritual and made that ritual holy. Whether we celebrate Holy Communion once a year or every Sunday, it is a vivid reminder that Jesus is alive, living inside each one of us. By the way, if you happen to be a person who has never taken Communion, don't think Christ can't live in you. It isn't a requirement—it's a beautiful sacrament.

What's a sacrament? It's a physical reminder—something you can see with your eyes—that helps you understand a wonderful truth you can't see.

If that's confusing, think about these examples. A wedding is a sign that two people are married. A baptism is a sign that somebody's ready to put Christ in charge of his or her life. A funeral is a sign that someone has died and we're saying good-bye.

Holidays can be signs too. They are holy days when . . .

- we think about God while we are celebrating them.
- we ask God to use our celebration as he wishes.
- we remember that these celebrations were initiated by God and we are privileged to take part in them.
- our celebration leaves us with an impression, almost like a footprint, that reminds us of the importance of the thing we're celebrating. So we remember not only the Easter eggs but also Jesus rising from the dead, not only dressing up like wise men but also God showing himself to us in a real, human life we can understand.

The best thing about holy days is that they don't just last for a day at a time. The Holy Spirit uses the lessons we learn all year long. If you celebrate Christmas with all its sacred symbols and you understand what Jesus' coming here was about, you're going to have Jesus on your mind all the time, reminding you of what kind of person he grew up to be and how you can grow up to be like him. With five days and seasons to celebrate, you're bound to be filled up with God all year long!

✓CHECK Yourself OUT

Maybe that all makes sense to you already and you want to go for it right now. Or you may be finding all this a little unsettling, because, frankly, you have always liked the egg hunt and the present opening just the way they are, thank you very much. Or it may be that you don't care a lot about holidays one way or the other, except for the fact that you don't have to do math on those days.

Before you read on, why not check out your current holiday 'tude. Choose the answer in each set of three that completes its statement in the way that is the most true for you (even if it doesn't describe you exactly). Be honest! There's no right or wrong reason—there is only you.

The first thing I think about when Thanksgiving is over and Christmas is on its way is . . .

a. _____there will be presents and a Christmas tree and stuff baking in the kitchen and my favorite Christmas songs and a huge turkey dinner.

b. _____I probably won't get what I want, my dad will be grouchy, and all my cousins are coming, and I'll have to entertain them.

c. _____we'll light the Advent candles and get the manger scene out and start Mary and Joseph on their journey and practice for the pageant at church.

When I start getting ready for Easter . . .

a. _____I want to shop for a new outfit and dye eggs and hope I'm not too old for an Easter basket, with those wonderful chocolate bunnies.

b. _____I don't want to go to church because my outfit is dumb, and I don't want any candy because I'll get fat, and I don't want to hide eggs for the little kids because I know I'll step in dog poop.

c. _____I can't wait to sing all those Christ-has-risen songs and see everything looking all colorful and newborn.

When Halloween rolls around . . .

a. _____I get my costume ready, make a new trick-or-treat bag, and beg my parents to let me go to the haunted house.

b. _____I wonder if I'm too old to wear a costume and go out trick or treating, and I dread those parties where they make you bob for apples and get your hair all wet.

c. _____I kind of ignore it because I'm not into ghosts and goblins and witches and all that other stuff that

Pick up a copy today at your local bookstore!

Softcover 0-310-70256-9

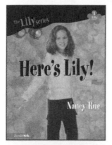

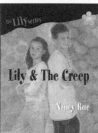

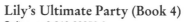
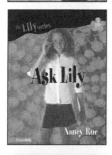
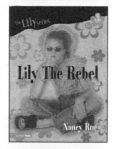

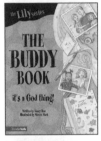

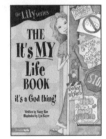

NIV Young Women of Faith Bible
GENERAL EDITOR SUSIE SHELLENBERGER

Designed just for girls ages 8-12, the *NIV Young Women of Faith Bible* not only has a trendy, cool look, it's packed with fun to read in-text features that spark interest, provide insight, highlight key foundational portions of Scripture, and more. Discover how to apply God's word to your everyday life with the *NIV Young Women of Faith Bible.*

Hardcover 0-310-91394-2

Softcover 0-310-70278-X

Slate Leather–Look™ 0-310-70485-5

Periwinkle Leather–Look™ 0-310-70486-3

Available now at your local bookstore!

Zonder**kidz**.

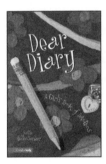

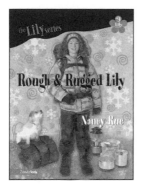
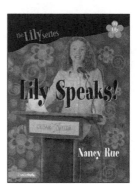

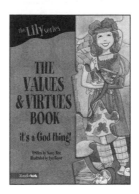

We want to hear from you. Please send your comments about this book to us in care of the address below. Thank you.

Zonderkidz.

Grand Rapids, MI 49530
www.zonderkidz.com